MURDER AND BUBBLY

A Cannoli Cafe Cozy Mystery

LIZZIE BENTON

http://lizziebenton.com

For my Family

CRIME SCENE

The guests at table eight spent the last hours of the year enjoying the food and each other's company. Nicole and Dean even got up to the dance floor for a few numbers. At ten minutes before midnight, the waitstaff poured sparkling wine in everyone's flutes, triggering the party guests to race back to their tables to prepare for the big moment. Tony took the microphone from the band leader and said, "Okay, everyone. It's that time! Here we go!"

"10...9...8...7...6...5...4...3...2...1...Happy New Year!" shouted the entire room. Everyone embraced one another while *Auld Lang Syne* played. Then, Tony announced for everyone to join him on the dance floor for some old Italian favorites. He asked the party guests to join hands while the band played the *Tarantella*. To Nicole's delight, a hundred people had huge smiles on their faces as they joined hands, rotated, and danced across the parquet floor together.

Nicole marveled at how huge the ballroom was, and its dance floor, to accommodate so many friends and family. It was simply magnificent to see so many happy people together in one place under gorgeous chandeliers, with a distant New York City as a backdrop. Often as she danced, she passed a "once removed cousin" here and a "second cousin" there, and in other instances she briefly passed people who must have known Tony well. After *That's Amore* played—with everyone holding each other and singing—Tony said it was time for a band break. It was just as well, since Nicole and her family were practically out of breath as they returned to their table. She was thinking about how everyone else must have also thirsted for both water and oxygen when she suddenly heard a loud shriek across the ballroom.

Everyone froze.

Dean was the first to move as he got into FBI mode and ran over to the back of the ballroom. Nicole followed close behind but was careful to let him take the lead. She noticed Dean stopped when he arrived at the back table where the Martini family had been sitting. She looked around to figure out what was going on and then suddenly realized everyone was looking down at the floor. When she followed their line of sight, she saw Phil Martini sprawled on the floor and gasped. Dean then leaned over and held his fingers on an exposed wrist. He sighed and announced, "He's dead!"

The whole room stayed silent as all the guests looked at one another, confused. Then she heard Dean tell people to "stay away from the blood on the carpet."

Nicole started to back away from the scene, feeling sick. She had just seen a body like this right before Christmas, and now it was happening again. Lia grabbed her arm and shook her head before whispering in her friend's ear, "I think you're right. He was hiding something...here we go again."

PROLOGUE

Two years ago, a minor earthquake hit the town of Rosewood, New Jersey. While there were no major injuries, it was a frightening incident, especially for a certain business mogul when one of the chandeliers started to fall in the ballroom of the mogul's establishment, the Rosewood Hotel, while he was standing underneath. The ground was vibrating so much, it was difficult for the old man to get his bearings. Fortunately, a young bellhop realized what was happening and helped move him to safety.

CHAPTER ONE

NICOLE TAPPED her foot under the table as she listened to the soft piano music. She wished she could make her foot tap to the beat of the tune, but she was a little too anxious for that. *What happened to him?* she wondered. In the past she wouldn't have minded being alone anywhere—in fact, she previously enjoyed a bit of solitude now and then—but given the recent events she endured, she had become a little more nervous.

Perhaps more than a *little*.

Dean had excused himself from the table to fetch wine from the cellar. She had not spent much time at Dean's house before—typically they ate out on their dates. But Dean said he had something special planned this evening and had even cooked for her—a first. When her eyes caught the two candlesticks before her, she realized he put a lot of thought into their date. Taking in a breath, she decided she needed to make a conscious effort to let go and savor the moment. She was *determined* to, in fact. After narrowly escaping yet another incident at gunpoint, which was becoming all too frequent since she returned to Rosewood, Nicole recognized that the quiet and peaceful time with Dean in that very moment was a rarity indeed and one to be treasured—if only she could get past her edginess.

Suddenly, there was a loud *pop* across the table. Nicole jumped as Dean uncorked the Prosecco. She looked over and blew out a breath of relief as he poured the bubbly into Nicole's flute and then his own. "I'm sorry, I should have given you notice. Didn't mean to scare you!"

"That's okay. I guess I'm still a little rattled by everything that happened last week." She rubbed the nape of her neck.

"It is understandable. Maybe I can help you focus on other things this evening." Raising his glass with a broad smile, he said, "To you, Nicole. The woman who inspires me to be better everyday."

Nicole felt her heart quicken as their eyes met— his soft, brown, soulful eyes. Maybe he would be successful in diverting her focus—he got her attention at least. They clinked glasses, and she didn't dare look away from those eyes—eyes that were stirring her feelings in a nervous yet pleasant way. "Thank you. And also, to you, Dean." Her voice shook. "If it hadn't been for you, I might not be here right now." She swallowed back the emotions rising up to her throat. "Thank goodness you're so sharp...that you understood my message."

Seated at a quaint table-for-two next to a roaring fire in Dean's home, Nicole raised her glass again and then sipped her Prosecco, enjoying the crisp taste in her mouth. She wasn't sure if it was introduction of the bubbly or the stronger presence —and conviction—she was sensing on Dean's part, but she felt her analytical and engineering mind begin to quiet; she was finally starting to relax.

"I don't want to lose you, Nicole. I just can't. I already—" His voice trailed off. Dean looked down and took a forkful of the chicken parmesan he had cooked for their special dinner. Nicole followed his lead and cut off a piece of the chicken, ensuring her sample had plenty of parmesan and gravy with it.

She saw his forehead crease and knew that look of pain. "This is delicious, Dean. I'm very impressed!" Nicole changed the subject, hoping that might help him feel better. She knew he was thinking about his beloved Jane—his wife—who suffered and passed away from cancer years before.

He raised his head and met her gaze again. "Nicole, I asked you here tonight because I wanted to have some more time with you, alone, without the whole town watching." He paused. "I need to tell you something."

Nicole cocked her head. "What is it?"

Dean shook his head and sighed. "I've been holding back. I want to share more and be more open with you, but I have been a little hesitant, and you have met me there." He set his fork down. "I *know* you hold back as well."

"Dean—" Nicole wanted to speak up, especially to explain the observation he made about her reserve, but he continued.

"But after this last incident, especially with your ex-fiance showing up, I feel more focused. I don't know how to explain it, but I think I need to demonstrate how much you mean to me. You need to know that you are absolutely amazing and that for the first time in years, I'm starting to feel alive again. I'm remembering who I am."

Nicole's eyes widened. She took Dean's hand

and noticed his eyes were moist. "It's funny, I actually feel exactly the same as you. You see, I was a bit reserved when we first got re-acquainted, around the time of the murder of the library director. And I was hesitant as we slowly dated. Not to mention that I had just acquired the Cannoli Cafe and was trying to figure out how to be a good owner and manager." Nicole squeezed his hand and leaned closer across the table. "But I'm finally starting to remember who I am, too—the Nicole deep-down—without the tarnish and hardening from the years in industry."

"You're a beautiful and kind person, Nicole. You never lost that. But I do think you had lost faith in people to a degree." Dean's eyebrows furrowed.

"I know. But I'm feeling better, especially now that I'm back in Rosewood. I love this community and finally feel I have a purpose, if nothing else than to help people enjoy a few minutes in the cafe. And seeing the kindness around me has helped restore my faith in others. You're helping to restore my faith, too." She smiled. "I appreciate how patient you've been. You know, as odd as that incident was last week, I've come to appreciate you and our relationship even more. It's so refreshing to be with you, someone who doesn't stifle my interests or tell me I'm doing too much with running the cafe or teaching part-time at the university, besides the fact that *you* are pretty unique."

"Oh, I am?" Dean laughed.

"Yes! How many private investigators do you know previously worked as an FBI agent, has a passion for gardening, and can draw pretty well?"

Dean smiled. "I guess I should cook for you more often! Keep it coming!" He chuckled. "Seriously, though, I am glad that we sneaked in this date. I'm sure tomorrow night will be a lot of fun celebrating New Year's Eve at such a big party, but there's no way we'll get any time alone there. And with the murder that just happened? Forget it. Everyone is going to flock to you! I know I'll be lucky if I even get once dance in with you."

"Wow, a dance—" Nicole glanced at the fire, thinking. "That would be nice. I don't think we've done that since—"

"The prom! I know! Crazy, right?" Dean kept looking at Nicole with a big smile.

"I can't believe that was almost twenty years ago, Dean. I'm so glad I returned to Rosewood...that we have a second chance, you know? And I'm glad we are being open about our feelings, that you broached this tonight."

Dean stood up, gently holding Nicole's hand. "May I have this dance?" Nicole realized the music had changed to a different tune and stood up in response to his question. Dean moved in close to her and whispered, "I feel the same." Her breathing became more shallow as she swayed with him. She could smell his cologne, a very clean scent, and closed her eyes.

Ring, ring, ring!

Dean's phone started to vibrate and ring loudly. Both Dean and Nicole jumped a little, a rousing summon out of their dreamy moment together.

"I'm so sorry, it's the chief. I have to get it."

Nicole nodded and broke away from him.

Dean answered. "Coogan speaking...Phil Martini's house...a break-in and attempted murder? I'll be right there."

CHAPTER TWO

"A PENNY FOR YOUR THOUGHTS?"

Nicole had been staring out the huge ballroom window when Lia interrupted her. The Rosewood Hotel stood elevated on the mountainous edge of town with New York City in the distance, producing beautiful, almost hypnotizing views, especially at night. This part of Rosewood bordered on the wealthy neighboring town of West Branford, and it wasn't far from the infamous Sycamore Street, where two murderers happened to live over the past year (prior to their arrests). From here, the center of Rosewood and the Cannoli Cafe seemed a little farther away. While most of the town's business operated around Main Street and the surrounding neighborhood, the town's economy did enjoy the benefit of the Rosewood Hotel sitting on its outskirts, especially when the hotel hosted conventions or provided rooms to business folks traveling to be near the city. Nicole flinched out of her daydream and turned around to address her best friend. "How would you account for the penny in your tax returns?"

"Funny! You do have a flair for humor, I'll give you that! Many other accountants would appreciate that joke, too!" Lia smiled at Nicole and grabbed her arm. "Come on, let's get some hors d'oeuvres. We need to get into the heart of the party. The servers keep passing you because your back is to the ballroom over here!"

"You're right. And the cocktail hour will be over before we know it!" Nicole scanned the room. It certainly was a festive party. A black-tie affair, she adored the old-fashioned nature of the event. Women in glamorous gowns, men in their tuxedos, servers pampering everyone with hors d'oeuvres and drinks—it was truly a delight. She couldn't help but wonder how long Dean would take to arrive though.

"Uh oh," Lia lamented. "I know that look. Nobody was murdered the last few days, so what *are* you thinking about?" Lia gave her friend a quizzical look and then turned her head quickly. "Oh, you have to try these." She pointed to a tray passing by with crab and gouda stuffed mushrooms.

The server must have overheard, because he turned around and offered the women napkins and frilled food picks before extending the tray in their direction. "Thank you," said Nicole. "These do look delicious!" The server caught her eye and smiled. Nicole suddenly felt a little self-conscious since he kept looking at her, hesitating to move on. Lia interrupted his moment and asked for another helping, prompting him to walk away after serving them.

"I can't blame him. You look absolutely stunning tonight, Nicole. If there was one good thing that came out of the last murder, it was that we got friendly with the victim's sister during the investigation. Who would have thought?" Lia wiped her fingers after finishing her second helping.

Nicole looked down at her red sequined gown, glittering with her every movement. "She did turn out to be quite helpful in the wardrobe department. I must say I like her boutique, and I think she will put the inheritance money to good use for her business." Nicole finished her stuffed mushroom and was ready to nibble on a few more delicacies before the formal dinner.

"The one who should really appreciate how you look is Dean. Where is he? He's awfully late. The cocktail hour is almost over!" Lia was heading to a food station featuring a raw food assortment and motioned for Nicole to follow her.

"He's helping the police chief on a case, actually. You know, we had a date last night—" started Nicole.

"Oh, pray tell!" Lia said in a high voice.

"It was very romantic. My heart is very taken by him, Lia." Nicole looked away from Lia's inquisitive hazel eyes, feeling vulnerable as she explained her date and her feelings. "I know we took things slowly since we got reacquainted, but the time has helped me really come to appreciate him...Last night was really special. He cooked for me at his house, and we talked about how we both want to focus more on our relationship..." Nicole's voice trailed off as her enthusiasm dropped into a frown.

Lia stopped walking in the direction of the station, her face brighter. "That's great! So why do you look upset?"

"We got interrupted. By a phone call from the chief," said Nicole. She rubbed her chin.

"Isn't that good? It seems like they are continuing to hire Dean as a private investigator. It looks like his business is doing well! You know me, the numbers are important!" She winked. "So what's the problem?"

"Dean is definitely more at ease now that he's had a steady stream of work coming in. He likes that he has more flexibility than if he worked there as a regular employee. That's for sure...but that's not the issue." Nicole's eyes furrowed as she started to whisper. "Lia, we were interrupted because there was a break-in and attempted murder at Phil Martini's house."

Lia gasped and put her hand over her mouth. "*The* Phil Martini? The owner of the Rosewood Hotel? Wait a second, isn't he here right now?"

"I think he is, yes! He's over there, in the back, with his wife Marjorie and a few of his associates, I suppose." Nicole gestured with her head in the business mogul's direction. He was well-known in New Jersey for owning the Rosewood Hotel as well as several other businesses.

"What do you know about the attempted murder then? This is interesting!" asked Lia in a hushed voice.

"So, the chief discounts his assumption that

someone tried to murder him, but that was the main reason Phil Martini called it in, it seems. *He* is the one calling the incident an attempted murder. He was convinced someone was going to kill him last night." Nicole shook her head. "But all they know is that someone rummaged through his home office, clearly looking for something, and escaped. He claims they took nothing, and the police believe him."

"Ah. *The police believe him*—there's the rub. So what does amateur sleuth Nicole think? This should be good," said Lia in a slightly mocking tone.

"Hey, my intuition is often right!" Nicole folded her arms.

Lia put her hand on Nicole's arm. "Okay, tell me."

Nicole, speaking quickly, explained, "I think he's hiding something. *I believe*, unlike the police, that something *was* stolen, something the police can't know about." Nicole nodded, emphasizing her point, as Lia's eyes widened. "You know why? It doesn't add up. Dean said the police were annoyed that he was practically saying *not* to look for the guy. On the one hand he wanted the intruder to get caught because he thought he was a murderer, but on the other hand he was acting like it didn't matter that there was a break-in and advised 'not to look too hard for him.'" Nicole put her fingers in the air, quoting him. "The whole thing sounds very odd."

"Well, here you are!" Nicole's father, John Capula, kissed his daughter as she and Lia both jumped, startled. "We thought we lost you!" Anna, Nicole's mother, was right behind him and put her arm around her daughter, smiling. Nicole glanced at Lia, her way of silently expressing that she'll fill her in on the rest of the details later. Lia's eyebrows gave the slightest twitch in response.

"No sign of Dean yet, sweetheart?" Aunt Lucia came around from the other side and kissed Nicole also.

"Not yet, but I'm sure he'll be here soon! Should we find our table?" asked Nicole.

"That sounds like a good idea. Tony said we're at table eight," said Nicole father.

"That's my name, don't wear it out!" said Tony, Nicole's second cousin (she believed he was her second cousin, at least; it was often hard for her to figure out if he was a second cousin or one of those 'once removed' cousins). A highly successful advertising executive in the city, Tony organized and hosted the annual New Year's Eve bash to bring relatives together along with some of his friends and business associates. Coincidentally—considering the events of the previous night—he was friends with Phil Martini who also happened to be the owner of the hotel, so Phil's family also attended the party—which included one of Nicole's Cannoli Cafe regulars, Don Martini of the Knights chess club.

"Hi Tony!" shouted everyone in unison. Nicole's family greeted him with hugs and kisses.

"Looks like another great bash, Tony! Thanks for having us again!" said Nicole's father.

"I'm just glad you could all make it! Too bad Stephen had to go back to Texas. Tell him to plan better next year! How could he miss this? What's wrong with that guy?" said Tony as he waved his hands in the air and shrugged his shoulders.

Everyone laughed at Tony's remark. He had that way of making everyone feel happy and comfortable, probably one of the reasons he was so good at his job. Nicole missed her brother, Stephen, as well, and hoped that he could visit New Jersey a bit more often in the future (or possibly even move back at some point).

"Listen, you guys enjoy, okay? The cocktail hour is over but we're going to step up the music now and before you know it you'll be eating prime rib!"

Nicole's family proceeded to table eight, which

was only a few feet away. Just as Nicole was about to sit down, she felt a tap on the shoulder.

"Umm, Professor, I just want to say hello," said Mr. Don Martini. There was a woman, perhaps ten to fifteen years younger than him, standing by his side.

Nicole thought about how she first came to know Mr. Martini, which was typically how she addressed him. Initially he was pretty grouchy with her, but over the past year he seemed to soften and now he was one of her biggest fans. He even seemed concerned for her safety when she found the body during the last murder incident in town. "Hello, Mr. Martini. How are you this evening?" She smiled at him, and also in the direction of his date, and then said, "Hello, I'm Nicole Capula. Mr. Martini plays chess some evenings in my cafe."

"It's so nice to meet you. I've heard so much about you, especially about how smart you are and that you teach at the University of New Jersey part-time! A Ph.D. chemical engineer *and* a former executive! My, you look so young to be so accomplished! My name is Clarisa Benhart."

Don spoke up, "I wanted to say hello to you, but I also came to get a break from my brother Phil. He's giving us all kinds of grief. Doesn't think I should be dating anyone, especially not anyone this beautiful. He should go back to worrying about his house break-in and leave me alone." Clarisa furrowed her eyebrows as she looked up to a scowling Don. "Now, don't you worry, Clarisa. I'll handle him. I've had enough of his nonsense." Don clenched his fists and gritted his teeth. Nicole could see he was trying very hard to restrain himself in front of Clarisa. She was pretty sure that he would be a lot more vocal and outwardly upset if he were with his chess buddies at the cafe, however.

Clarisa contorted her face and Nicole sympathized, realizing she must have felt quite embarrassed by the talk. She was about to change the subject when Dean turned up.

"Nicole, I made it! Wow, you look absolutely gorgeous." He paused as he admired his New Year's date.

"I agree!" said Don Martini. Clarisa nudged him along and then he said, "Enjoy the evening!"

Dean wore a striking black tuxedo. She also noticed he was wearing contact lenses instead of his usual glasses, showing off his warm brown eyes. Nicole thought he was simply debonair as they say. "Here, let me help you." Dean pulled the chair out for her before sitting down. Her family greeted him warmly, and then a dish of classic shrimp cocktail was placed before each person.

"I'm heading to the bar to get a mixed drink," said Lia. "Anyone need anything?"

Everyone replied that they were fine with the wine on the table except for Aunt Lucia. "I'll have a martini. Gin with three olives!" Lia nodded and started to walk away when Aunt Lucia shouted, "Don't let them forget the olives!" Everyone chuckled.

Dean whispered to Nicole, "Lia is included in all your family's events? I know she's your best friend, but...where is her family? You two never talk about them, and I've always been afraid to ask. Are they on the outs with each other or something?"

Nicole set her fork down and pressed her lips together before answering. "Lia's parents were tragically killed when she was abroad studying for her international MBA years ago."

"Oh my goodness! I had no idea! I guess I missed that, maybe when I was down in Washington," Dean rubbed his forehead.

"I will explain more another time. But they were killed in a severe car accident. Ever since, my parents have always extended invitations to Lia, especially because they were close friends, her parents and mine."

Lia returned with two martinis, one for Aunt Lucia and one for herself. "Thank you, my dear. Great minds think alike, I see!" Everyone laughed again at Aunt Lucia's remarks.

The guests at table eight spent the last hours of the year enjoying the food and each other's company. Nicole and Dean even got up to the dance floor for a few numbers. At ten minutes before midnight the waitstaff poured sparkling wine in everyone's flutes, triggering the party guests to race back to their tables to prepare for the big moment. Tony took the microphone from the band leader and said, "Okay, everyone. It's that time! Here we go!"

"10...9...8...7...6...5...4...3...2...1...Happy New Year!" shouted the entire room. Everyone embraced one another while *Auld Lang Syne* played. Then, Tony announced for everyone to join him on the dance floor for some old Italian favorites. He asked everyone to join hands while the band played the *Tarantella*. To Nicole's delight, a hundred people had huge smiles on their faces as they joined hands, rotated, and danced across the parquet floor together.

Nicole marveled at how huge the ballroom was, and its dance floor, to accommodate so many friends and family. It was simply magnificent to see so many happy people together in one place under gorgeous chandeliers, with a distant New York City as a backdrop. Often as she danced, she passed a "once removed cousin" here and a "second cousin" there, and in other instances she briefly passed people who must have known Tony well. After *That's Amore* played—with everyone holding each other and singing—Tony said it was time for a band break. It was just as well, since Nicole and her family were practically out of breath as they returned to their table. She was thinking about how everyone else must have also thirsted for both water and oxygen when she suddenly heard a loud shriek across the ballroom.

Everyone froze.

Dean was the first to move as he got into FBI mode and ran over to the back of the ballroom. Nicole followed close behind but was careful to let him take the lead. She noticed Dean stopped when he arrived at the back table where the Martini family had been sitting. She looked around to figure out what was going on and then suddenly realized everyone was looking down at the floor. When she followed their line of sight, she saw Phil Martini sprawled on the floor and gasped. Dean then leaned over and held his fingers on an exposed wrist. He sighed and announced, "He's dead!"

The whole room stayed silent as all the guests looked at one another, confused. Then she heard Dean tell people to "stay away from the blood on the carpet."

Nicole started to back away from the scene, feeling sick. She had just seen a body like this right before Christmas, and now it was happening again. Lia grabbed her arm and shook her head before whispering in her friend's ear, "I think you're right. He was hiding something...here we go again."

CHAPTER THREE

NICOLE AWOKE to the sound of Ringo barking.

Woof, woof, woof!

She groaned. It was 8 a.m. on New Year's Day, and she had only been sleeping for a few hours. The police had detained the party guests half the night to investigate Phil Martini's murder, and she was absolutely exhausted.

Ring, ring! Woof, woof!

"Oh, the doorbell. Yikes." She realized her black labrador retriever probably sensed someone approaching the door. She struggled to pull herself out of bed, her limbs feeling heavy, and pulled her robe over her new satin pajamas as best she could.

She approached the front door and looked into the peephole. "Lia! Oh my goodness!" Nicole opened the door and said, "What are you doing here? Not again!"

"Coming through. You know the routine by now, Nicole! Any time there is a murder, I stay over." Lia gently pushed her way past Nicole, rolling her luggage behind her.

"But it's only eight in the morning!" She sighed.

Woof, woof!

"See, Ringo knows the routine! How are you, boy? Aunt Lia is back!" Lia rubbed his head. He panted in delight and stayed by her side.

"Here we go again. Okay, you win. Coffee or tea?" Nicole tightened her robe around her, feeling cold and too tired to argue with her friend. "Guess I'm making breakfast now."

"Actually, I brought egg sandwiches from that franchise doughnut shop. Figured you needed a break." Lia handed her a paper back. "We just need coffee."

"Did you get doughnuts, too?" asked Nicole as she accepted the bag and proceeded into the kitchen.

"No, was I supposed to? I didn't think you'd want them since you usually have cannolis." Lia arched her eyebrows.

"Actually, I don't have any now. We closed early

yesterday and we won't reopen until tomorrow. Susie worked it out so that we would use up our inventory and have a clean start for the new year."

"You guys are thinking like accountants, very good!" Lia nodded approvingly and then wiggled the handle on her luggage. "I'll go put this around the corner while you put the coffee on. Nice jammies, by the way."

"Jammies? Oh, these were a gift from my mom." Nicole marveled at how Lia had so much energy that morning. She, however, felt so depleted after everything they had been through. Instead of going home after the festivities, they had to wait around all night while the police interviewed guests and sifted out potential suspects. That was another thing—the suspect they had identified so far. She knew Don Martini must have been very upset about his brother's murder, but on top of his grief, the police were asking him a lot of questions. Don had told the police he was in the bathroom at the time of the murder, but no one can confirm that. There were also reports from party guests at their table and the surrounding tables that they argued a lot that night. He had even said so to Nicole when the dinner started. Don Martini was a grouchy old man sometimes, but capable of murder? That she wasn't so sure of.

"Where's the joe?" Lia was back and perkier than ever. She put her pen and legal pad on the table, clearly ready to start sleuthing.

"Sorry, I was thinking about something." Nicole opened her cabinet and retrieved two mugs before hitting the buttons on her single-serve coffee maker. Meanwhile, Lia helped herself to two plates and placed their egg sandwiches on them.

"I know you have a soft spot for that old Mr. Martini. That's it, right?" Lia asked as she pulled up a chair at the kitchen table.

"You know me too well, Lia." Nicole sighed. "I just hope the police can narrow down the right people this time." Nicole brought the filled mugs over to the table. "Here, I have French vanilla creamer."

"Thanks." Lia poured and stirred the creamer in her mug. "Is Dean involved? Maybe if they put him on the homicide cases they would actually get somewhere."

"Dean continues to help them with their backlog or things like burglaries, etc. Basically, they employ Dean almost like a contractor, plus he has other clients he supports. The chief of police appreciated his help in terms of some of the crisis management last night, but he's not supposed to get in the way of the homicide detectives. Instead, they want him to take the burden off the force by handling some of the other crimes." Nicole took a bite of her sandwich and was pleasantly surprised at how good it tasted.

"So what are you going to do about it? I know you have a plan brewing in your head, Nicole."

Nicole's eyes widened when Lia shot her a look. "I don't know, honestly. I still feel like I accidentally solved those cases that happened last year, mostly because I wound up in the wrong place at the wrong time...you know, like at gunpoint. I would like to avoid that again, but at the same time I never feel anyone is looking in the right places."

Nicole noticed Lia squint her eyes, as if she was deep in thought. "I think you need to trust yourself a little more. It wasn't an accident that you wound up at gunpoint on those occasions. You found yourself in those situations because you eliminated the other suspects essentially. I think you should nurture your sleuthing skills, actually."

"What? But then I might be put in harm's way?" Nicole wrinkled her forehead.

"You can't help being so intrigued anyway. So might as well get good at detective work. I think your analytical skills can be put to good use—informally, of course. Besides, I have an ulterior motive." Lia's eyes turned red.

Nicole looked at her friend and wondered what Lia was getting at.

Ring, ring, ring!

Suddenly, the house phone was ringing. Nicole and Lia looked at each other. "That's weird, no one ever calls me on my landline." It rang a few more times. Ringo started barking before Nicole stood up to reach for it. "Hello?" Nicole heard a woman's voice on the other end. "Yes, this is she...he is asking for me?" Nicole made the motion of writing in air to Lia, who then handed her the pen and paper from the kitchen table. "Actually, I have company right now, my friend Lia. I hope it's okay if she visits with me...Can you tell me the address?" Nicole quickly wrote it down. "Got it. We'll be there in an hour." She hung up the phone and didn't say anything.

"Earth to Nicole? Where are we going?" asked Lia.

"That was Clarisa, Don's date from last night. She said Don's in a bad state and keeps mumbling that he needs to speak to me. She asked if we could come over."

"Hmm. Let the sleuthing begin."

CHAPTER FOUR

AFTER SWALLOWING down the remainder of their egg sandwiches and draining their coffee mugs, Nicole and Lia quickly prepared for their departure to Mr. Martini's house. It wasn't far, but Nicole felt unkempt after not really sleeping the night before. Lia may have complimented Nicole on her satin pajamas, but Nicole felt her face and her hair needed *quite* a bit of refreshing.

Lia had offered to take Ringo out while Nicole freshened up, and for that she was very grateful. While she was used to living alone for many years—everywhere from Texas to Oakwood (a town conveniently near the University of New Jersey and within commuting distance of her former job at LMKJ Chemical)—she had started to enjoy having company, especially Lia, around on and off the last year. Of course, Lia only showed up when there was a murder, plus she happened to live around the corner—quite convenient for their friendship indeed. But it got Nicole thinking about her future. If she and Dean continued down a serious path, would it lead to marriage and sharing a house together? And whose house would they live in— hers or his, or would they buy a new one? She winced at the thought, for she loved her current one. Nicole shook her head to herself as she rinsed out the conditioner from her hair. *Don't be so silly, get back to the murder*, she scolded herself.

Once Nicole wrapped herself in a towel and looked in the mirror, she breathed out a small sigh of relief that the shower did improve her appearance slightly, at least making her look clean. She would accept any improvement she could get. On top of that, she felt a little more energetic after her egg sandwich and coffee. And Lia's arrival. *Maybe it was good that Lia turned up after all,* Nicole thought. She could help her get a jump on the biggest question on her mind—who murdered Phil Martini, and why?

After Nicole blew her hair dry, using mousse to neaten the waves throughout, she put on a pair of dressy jeans with a burgundy cowl neck sweater. As she quickly applied her makeup, she shouted down the hall, "I'm almost done!" She wasn't sure if Lia heard her but she at least wanted her friend to know, in case she hadn't taken Ringo out yet.

When Nicole went to grab her bag, she realized she had most of her valuables still inside her small dress bag from the night before. She quickly transferred the contents to her typical everyday black tote bag and briskly returned to the living room, worried she left Lia waiting too long. When she arrived in the living room, however, she found her friend staring at the television, thoroughly engrossed in whatever she was viewing. "What's this?"

"This is one of those murder mystery movies. I'm watching for tips. I think the wife did it!" said Lia.

"In the movie or do you mean Phil Martini's wife, Marjorie?" asked Nicole. "Because I've been wondering about her. Does anybody know anything about her? She is very private."

"The movie. But now that you mention it...where was she last night?" asked Lia. "I didn't see her, but I thought she was the one who screamed. That would mean she must have been dancing with the rest of us when he was shot, right?"

"That remains to be seen. Let's see if Don can shed any light when we visit him."

Lia parked her Mercedes-Benz SUV in front of a beautiful Victorian house. Nicole immediately knew that this was one of the first homes built in Rosewood, which started as a vacation town in the early 1900s. Homes like Don Martini's often enjoyed the river running behind it, which also ran through the town. Unlike his brother, Don lived around the corner from Main Street, and she knew he typically walked the couple blocks to her cafe with his buddy Max. But that was the difference between Don and Phil. Though she barely knew the deceased owner of the Rosewood Hotel, she was keenly aware that Don was more the type to socialize in the community (despite his grumpy facade). Phil Martini, however, often acted like he was above it, and though no one could blame him for wanting to live in a mansion in the mountainous area by the hotel, he certainly didn't appear interested in what the rest of the community had to offer.

"What a nice Christmas present to yourself. This car is gorgeous. Congratulations!" said Nicole. "I have to admit I'm surprised, though. You're always talking about how cars depreciate the second they are off the lot. What happened? Did the murders convince you that life is too short?" asked Nicole.

"Thanks." Lia sighed. "I know, I went against my own advice. But I don't see anything changing in my life too soon. No Dean in my life. And my parents didn't live long, you know. Figured maybe it was time to splurge on myself for a change. Besides, I have been offering to travel for my high-end clients so I did get to count it as a business expense." Lia let out a hearty chuckle before her expression turned. "Speaking of my..." Her voice trailed off as her eyes widened. Nicole turned her head toward Don Martini's house and her jaw dropped.

Nicole quickly got out of the car. "Mr. Martini!" She saw the grouchy old man in a bathrobe and slippers running toward her in the cold.

"He did it. I know he did. You have to get him, Professor. But the police don't believe me. Please, you have to help me. Talk to Dean!" shouted Mr. Martini. Out of the corner of Nicole's eye she saw a few neighbors come out to see what all the commotion was about. She turned around and caught Lia's eye. She grabbed one arm and Lia grabbed the other.

"Let's go, Mr. Martini. Let's warm up inside and we can talk all about it."

CHAPTER FIVE

NICOLE AND LIA struggled as they practically dragged Mr. Don Martini back into his own home as he ranted and raved about his brother's murder. Nicole, red-faced from the consequential embarrassment outside, spotted his new companion Clarisa in the doorway. Clarisa opened the door and called, "Come inside, Don, please! Listen to the bright women. It will all be better soon." After spotting his new love, Don acquiesced and finally carried his weight as the three of them made their way into his beautiful, historic home.

Clarisa offered to take their coats and then asked them to sit in the living room. Nicole was pleased to see a tray of tea and biscuits waiting on the coffee table. After everything they just went through, she was ready to accept any kind of fortification offered to her.

Don had been pacing back and forth since they first walked in. He finally sat down in a chair near the coffee table while Nicole and Lia found their seats on the sofa. Clarisa sat down in an accent chair near them, the lines in her face softer now that they were no longer dragging Don in from the outside. "Please, help yourselves. And thank you both for coming. Lia, I didn't get to meet you last night but I've heard so much about you, too."

Lia smiled after pouring tea for herself and Nicole. "It's nice to meet you, too. And Happy New Year!"

Everyone looked at each other.

Nicole noticed the look of despair on Don's face. "I suppose we all nearly forgot about the holiday. Maybe once we can figure out who murdered Phil, we can at least move on, though I am very sorry for your loss, Mr. Martini."

"Please, call me Don from now on. I know I gave you a hard time at first, but playing chess in your cafe gives me something to look forward to every week, and I am grateful." Clarisa looked over at Nicole and smiled, clearly seeming pleased that Don's mood had improved.

"And please call me, Nicole." She smiled warmly at him. "I don't want to upset you, but it sounds like you want to discuss what happened last night. Is there anything you can tell us?" Nicole pressed her lips together, wondering what he was referring to outside. She saw Lia take her paper and pen out from her bag. If someone hadn't actually died, Nicole probably would have chuckled at the fact that they nearly appeared like a real detective team, with a designated note-taker and all.

Don sat up in his chair. "I was in the bathroom last night when someone shot my brother." He shook his head and looked down. "Unfortunately, the murderer used a silencer, otherwise someone might have heard the shot from the hallway."

Nicole took a sip of her tea. "What about right before that? What do you remember?"

"Well, we all said Happy New Year, but Phil and I stayed at the table after that. We had even remarked on the fact that we're old men and actually laughed about it." Don's voice lifted momentarily and the corners of his lips turned up just a bit. "So we didn't go up to the dance floor when the rest of you were up there." *Too bad no one heard them laughing*, Nicole thought. *The guests only noticed when they argued.*

"Except for me. I was up on the dance floor, and I was the one who screamed when I returned. I left Don and Phil at their seats for a while." Clarisa nodded. Nicole figured she was making a point, that she wasn't near them for some time—particularly when the murder occurred.

"But the police think I did it. They said witnesses heard us arguing a lot last night and that it's a reason to suspect me," Don stopped, a tear going down his face. "He was a pain in the neck, but he was *my* pain in the neck. He was *my* brother. Mine! And I would rather be here arguing with him than have him dead!" Don buried his face in his hands, sobbing. Clarisa stood up and put her arm around him.

Everyone stayed quiet while Don grieved. Nicole gave Clarisa a sympathetic look while she tried to calm Don down.

Finally, Lia broke the silence. "Don't they have cameras at the hotel that can prove you weren't around when it happened?" Nicole felt that it was a good question and was glad Lia had asked it. She knew the police were confused last night, thinking there had to be hidden cameras somewhere, since nothing was obvious. But the hotel staff kept pointing the finger at the next employee, not knowing the answer. Maybe at least Don knew how his brother operated the hotel in terms of security. Or maybe that's why he was a suspect in the view of the police, that he could have insider knowledge.

Don looked up, wiping his nose with a tissue that Clarisa had handed him. "Let's just say my brother didn't always do things on the up and up. He had some deals going on in the background and didn't want traceability. He had a lot of meetings at the hotel and didn't want any footage." Don shook his head. "But he never considered maybe it would have deterred someone from committing a crime against him, or taking his life!"

That got Nicole thinking. "Did he have any cameras at his own house or did he do deals there, too?" Nicole nearly surprised herself when she said the word *deals*. They were starting to sound like a pair of crime detectives.

"Same thing. He didn't like the idea of cameras," Don said. "But I know who broke into his place, or at least appeared to."

Both Nicole and Lia flinched. "Who?" asked Nicole. *And what did he mean by appeared to*, she wondered.

"The same person who drove Marjorie home last night. She left early at 11 p.m., complaining of a headache. I told the police to check them both out, actually, but they don't believe me."

Lia looked at Nicole, probably to see if she knew what Don was talking about. Nicole didn't recall Dean mentioning anything, but she hardly got to speak with him last night. Besides, maybe Don didn't say anything to them until he was at the police station in the wee hours of the morning, after they finished interviewing guests at the hotel. Nicole realized Don had probably just gotten home when Clarisa called and considered how absolutely exhausted he must have been feeling.

"Who drove her home, Mr. Martini...I mean, Don?" asked Nicole.

"She called her best friend, Jeannette Pierson." Don's fatigue was starting to show. His eyes started to close and his words sounded a bit slurred.

"So you think this Jeannette Pierson broke into Phil's house? Then who is the man who murdered him?"

Don was fading in his chair. He put his head back and said, "I'm sorry, I can barely stay awake. Clarisa, call my doctor. He needs to check my meds." He closed his eyes, and Lia gave Nicole a panicked look. Nicole was desperate to at least get the name of the person Don suspected. Maybe if they could investigate that person, in addition to Jeannette, they might get somewhere.

"Don, I'm sorry. One last question. The man...who do you think murdered Phil?" Nicole stood up to get closer to Don, hoping he could utter one or more two words. Clarisa walked away quickly and got her cell phone.

"Her husband." And with that, Don completely passed out.

CHAPTER SIX

"I CAN'T BELIEVE THIS. Poor Mr. Martini!" said Nicole. They waited in Lia's car as the paramedics rolled Mr. Don Martini into the ambulance.

"He'll be okay. He's probably dehydrated and this much stress isn't good for him." Nicole thought about the phone conversation Clarisa exchanged with the doctor. She explained how he started to drift off and that once he passed out, they couldn't wake him. The doctor told her to call for help immediately.

"I'm just glad that he had a pulse. I can't handle another dead body!" Nicole closed her eyes and rested her head in her hand against the window.

"Okay, Clarisa just got in the back and they closed the doors." Lia paused. "Now they are pulling away. How about we go home and take a nap. Don't we have dinner at your parents' tonight?" asked Lia.

"You're right. I keep forgetting it's New Year's Day. I wanted to figure out this Jeannette Pierson angle, but we should get some rest first. Hopefully we can hit the ground running tomorrow. Also, maybe Dean will have some information for us this evening."

"He'd better!" said Lia.

Nicole sipped on the red vermouth in her parents' living room, still worried about Mr. Martini. Lia came in from the hallway with a big smile on her face.

"Great news! He was dehydrated, as I suspected. I gave Clarisa my number earlier and she just called me with the update." Lia wiped her forehead, clearly relieved. "They will keep him a few days for observation and they are loading him up with IV fluids."

"What about his heart? Is he okay? I think he's on heart meds," said Nicole.

"That's right, she did mention that his EKG

didn't look normal, probably from the stress. But his heart is okay."

Nicole nodded. "Good, I hope he'll be alright. Now I really feel I need to solve this case! Mr. Martini deserves that much!"

"Excuse me, young lady? You're going to do what?" Nicole's father, John, appeared in the doorway. "Now, don't you remember what happened the last time you tried to solve a case? We almost lost you!" His jaw tightened. She recognized that look from her childhood, but hadn't seen it in a long time. At least she was still a young lady in his view.

"I just mean I wish I could reduce his emotional pain. I know he's grieving, but he's also feeling burdened since he's considered a suspect. And he seems to know who murdered his brother but can't prove it." She took another sip of her drink. "Now that he's in the hospital we probably shouldn't pepper him for information." Nicole looked over at Lia, thinking about when they dealt with Aunt Lucia's hospitalization during the investigation of the murder of the library director. She finished the rest of her vermouth and put the glass down on the coaster. Just then she heard a knock at the door.

"I'll get it," offered Lia. When Dean walked in, Nicole's mother Anna appeared in the hallway to take his coat. He thanked her and then presented her with a bottle of Prosecco.

"Thank you, Dean. This will be perfect for our New Year's toast." She smiled and turned to the living room. "Let's sit in the dining room. We're ready!"

When they all sat down, Dean remarked on how wonderful their feast looked. Nicole's mom had prepared an Italian pot roast. Nicole eyed the roast that still had foil around it, to keep it warm, and couldn't wait for them to dig in. She was absolutely starving after working up an appetite earlier that day.

Nicole's father popped open the Prosecco and started pouring it for each person at the table, while Nicole's mother brought out the appetizer— Roasted Asparagus Wrapped in Prosciutto.

"I'm sorry, Mom, I should be helping you. Do you need anything?" Nicole shook her head to herself. "I'm just so preoccupied from everything last night, and with what happened at Mr. Martini's house."

"Just enjoy tonight. I know you have a big day tomorrow reopening the cafe." Nicole's mother, Anna, had a soft voice and a very gentle way about her. Now a retired kindergarten teacher, she enjoyed spending her time reading historical fiction and cooking and baking new recipes. She tended to encourage Nicole's independence and gave her the space she needed at times, yet she was very warm and caring with her. The combination was possibly one of the reasons Nicole was so accomplished in her life.

Her father, on the other hand, could be stern at times, though he had softened in his retirement from working as refinery superintendent. "Before we discuss last night, since I suspect that's what's on everyone's mind, let's do a quick toast." Anna stood next to her husband as he raised his glass. "Anna and I wish everyone a very Happy and Healthy New Year!" Dean, Nicole, and Lia all stood up and clinked their glasses with one another.

After sitting down and taking a bite of the asparagus, Nicole's father John said, "Okay, Dean. What are you allowed to tell us about the murder?"

Nicole looked over to her beau to her right and saw his cheeks flush a little. She knew these family events were a little stressful for him, but he always handled himself with poise—with the minor exception being the incident before Christmas when Nicole's ex-fiance turned up.

"Truthfully, the police don't know much more

than you do. I'm not officially on it, as you know. But, the chief and others like to talk to me and sometimes get my opinion." Dean took a bite of his asparagus. "This is very good, Mrs. Capula." She smiled in return.

"So what is your opinion, pray tell?" asked John in a strong voice. Nicole could see her father was putting more pressure on Dean. Though her father didn't say it outright, she knew what he was getting at. He didn't care who was assigned to the case, he just thought Dean should be the one doing the investigating and not his daughter!

Nicole glanced across the table at her friend and Lia gave the slightest wince, clearly picking up on what was going on at the table. She shifted her eyes in Dean's direction and saw his face turn a few shades redder.

Dean swallowed. "The problem is, Phil Martini was so well-known. We have no idea what the motive could have been for his murder. As a starting point, I suggested that they investigate anything abnormal that happened at the party, in addition to the people working at the hotel." He sighed. "The other issue is that anyone could have come in off the street and posed as a party guest. This investigation could take months, or years. It might even become a cold case, it's that big and wide with no clear enemies or motives."

"Guess I'm staying at your house for good, Nicole!" Lia chuckled.

Nicole ignored her friend's comment. "But what about Mr. Martini? I mean Don. Why is he a suspect? And what about the people he said to investigate?" asked Nicole. She cocked her head, anxious to hear Dean's answer.

"He is a person of interest, yes. My under-standing is that the police had to do their due dili-gence because several people witnessed an extremely heated conversation between Don and his brother, to the point where Don banged his fists on the table and walked out of the ballroom at one point. The guests said that was before midnight, so some speculated that he left, got his gun, and returned." Dean paused. "Of course, we don't know yet if he owned a gun, or where he would have access to one. That's being looked at."

"But Jeannette Pierson and her husband? For some reason Don believes they had something to do with the break-in and murder?" Nicole looked at Dean with pleading eyes, a little more biased than she is normally—ready to protect her dear Mr. Martini.

Dean shook his head. "He said that, but we have no proof of anything. Jeannette picked up her friend, Marjorie—Phil's wife—around 11 p.m. That's consistent with the time guests saw her leave." Dean arched his eyebrows. "But there is no connection to Jeannette or her husband except that Marjorie is close friends with her."

Nicole's dad piped up, squinting his eyes in thought. "What about going through his records and all that?" Anna's mother stood up and collected the appetizer plates while the lively discussion continued. She then took the foil off and started serving pieces of the pot roast on each person's plate.

"They are getting all that through Phil's operations manager, Al Roman. Apparently, he keeps track of the records."

John took a bite of the pot roast and washed it down with the rest of his Prosecco. Then he poured red wine in his glass. "So how are you going to make sure my daughter doesn't get involved. Can you take her out, away from all this?" Nicole and Lia looked at each other.

"Well, I actually have an announcement to make." Lia moved up on the edge of her seat as Dean spoke. "I'm taking an art class at the community college in the coming semester. To help prepare, the instructor wants us to attend the art show at the Pierson Gallery tomorrow night. Nicole, would you like to join me?" asked Dean.

"Wait just a second here. Pierson? As in the couple you were just speaking of?" asked John.

"Yes, they own the gallery, but they don't have any connection to the murder. This is supposed to be a fun event," said Dean.

John shook his head. "I don't like it. Something isn't right about all this. Nicole seems to trust her Mr. Martini. He may be onto something...Dean, you make sure nothing happens to her! And what's this about the art?" Nicole saw her father clench his fist. She realized that she had underestimated how affected he was by the last murder incident in town.

"Oh, Dean is a wonderful artist, Dad! You should see some of his drawings. I've been encouraging him on and off the past year to do more with his talent. Glad he's taking my advice!" Dean smiled at Nicole. "Yes, I would love to go!" Of course, Nicole had an ulterior motive in this—she could possibly look into Mr. Martini's assertion during her date. But she had also recognized Dean's support in her interests in their relationship and was trying to make an effort to support his as well in the recent months.

Nicole looked over at Lia, who had sunk in her chair. She was clearly disappointed that the announcement was not about an engagement but instead concerning an art class.

The rest of the dinner was a little less tense, with talk of reopening the cafe the next day and plans for the Capulas to return to their other home in Texas in a few weeks. Nicole was in a better mood, too. After seeing Don in the morning, she wasn't sure how she was going to investigate his claim, but Dean happened to solve that for her quite easily with their new plans to visit the art gallery.

Maybe it would be a great year after all— once all this trouble was over.

CHAPTER SEVEN

NICOLE ARRIVED at the Cannoli Cafe at 5 a.m. on January 2nd. When she parked in the back lot behind the cafe, she noticed one other car there— Susie's. "Thank goodness. I really need her help today," she muttered to herself as she put her car in park.

Susie was one of the most reliable people Nicole had ever met, and that included all the individuals she worked with previously in the chemical industry and at the university. Besides Susie being an extremely conscientious person, a wonderful baker, and a great manager (a role she naturally grew into over the past year), she also happened to be one of the kindest and warmest people Nicole had ever met. Nicole was also surprised how many hours

Susie wanted to work at the cafe, but she also knew Susie did not have much family around anymore. After Susie had given birth to her daughter, Michelle, Susie's husband had been killed. He was a police detective in New Cove and got caught in the crossfire when he was hunting down a prominent drug dealer in the city's "underworld." His work led him to earn a posthumous medal, since his distinct work on the case led to the dealer's capture, but his wife and daughter lost their beloved pillar of the family. Susie managed for a few years on life insurance and benefits due to the nature of his death. As Michelle got older, Susie got more involved with the town and started working at the Rosewood Coffee Shoppe, owned by Bert Davison. Eventually, Bernadette, the previous owner of the Cannoli Cafe, caught on to how efficient and reliable Susie was and lured her away from Bert's establishment by offering her double the pay and more hours— exactly what Susie wanted, especially once her daughter relocated to California for a job. By the time Bernadette had passed away and bequeathed the cafe to Nicole, Susie had enough experience to help Nicole in the transition, which she seemed very happy to do. She often wondered if Susie would have preferred to own it, and had even wondered if she should make her a partner in the future, but Susie always said she enjoyed running the cafe without the responsibility of actually owning it at the end of the day. It helped her sleep at night, plus she was still trying to figure out if she would stay in New Jersey or relocate to California, if her daughter decided to remain there.

When Nicole opened the back door and walked in, she smelled the wonderful aroma of coffee brewing and cookies baking. Susie walked briskly to the back. "Happy New Year, dear!" She gave Nicole a big hug and seemed genuinely excited to see her.

"Happy New Year, Susie!" Nicole smiled at her capable baker. "Wow, smells great in here. I think I'll have a cup of coffee when it finishes brewing." Nicole started to remove her coat and bag and placed them in her little cubicle area in the back of the kitchen.

"I'll get it for you, dear. And I also have the cookies in the oven, and the cannoli shells are ready to be filled," said Susie.

"You really are the best, Susie. I truly don't know what I'd do without you. If there is anything I can do to make things easier for you, please let me know. I don't want you to think I'm taking advantage!"

Susie brought over a cup with fresh coffee and offered Nicole the creamer. "Well, actually, there's been a new development."

"Oh?" Nicole stirred in the creamer and returned it to Susie. Was Susie going to move to California after all?

"My daughter, Michelle, got engaged to someone she met in California! He's a wonderful guy. She brought him home for the holidays so I could meet him!"

"That's fantastic! Congratulations!" Nicole set her coffee down and gave Susie a hug. "Oh, is there bad news then? I guess I'm losing you to California?"

"Believe it or not, they plan to move here! They do want to have the wedding out in California, but her fiance, Josh, is in finance and will be accepting a promotion at his company to transfer to the New York City location!"

"Wow, so you don't have to move?" asked Nicole.

"No...but I was thinking that I'd like to reduce my hours, since I'd like to spend more time with my daughter once she's back." Susie paused and pressed her lips together, clearly waiting to see Nicole's reaction.

"I think that makes sense. What do you have in mind? I was already thinking of bringing Lia on board to keep track of our books, so that we would spend less time poring over them. I know she handles the end of the year taxes and all, but I think we need more help with the day-to-day stuff."

"Oh, yes, that would be wonderful! In fact, that's exactly what I was thinking...I'd like to focus on my strong points and what I enjoy doing most. I actually love coming in early every day to do the baking, and I would like to be able to leave at 2 p.m. to get the rest of the day to myself." She hesitated. "But I know you teach classes sometimes, and you shouldn't have to be here all the time as the owner."

"So we should probably hire someone to help with the front, right? Maybe to handle customers at the register and wait on them?" asked Nicole. She took another sip of her coffee, enjoying the smooth yet bright flavor.

"Yes, that would be great. I have to tell you— since you took over, business has been booming and from what I remember after looking at the books at the end of the year, we definitely can afford to retain Lia and hire help."

"Yes, I thought so too, when I saw the numbers and that's when I started to consider expanding our staff." Nicole bit her lip. "Also, Dean and I were talking before New Year's, and we agreed we should focus more on our relationship. I do want to give it a shot with Dean. I am hopeful to have a future with him...I've been spread thin between being here, teaching at the university—"

Susie interrupted her. "And solving murder crimes!" She waved her finger in the air. "Oh, you need to tell me what happened at that party when you're done, dear! It's all over the news about Phil Martini's murder!"

Nicole felt a little startled that Susie had raised her voice in excitement—she normally seemed so calm and steady. "I was just going to say I am completely on board with hiring help. We both need to have better balance in our lives." Nicole nodded, emphasizing her point. "And I am ready to solve another murder, actually! I feel so bad for Don Martini. I honestly don't think he did it, yet he's the lead suspect right now!"

Susie's lips formed a small smile. "Don't worry, Nicole. You *know* your regulars will be a fountain of information today when we open. Well, I'm glad we had this talk. Maybe we'd better finish preparing the baked goods for the front. I have a feeling we will be pretty swamped today," she said, raising her eyebrows.

Nicole and Susie spent the remaining time preparing the cafe for rush hour. Sure enough, Rosewood was back to normal in terms of its work schedule. As usual, people came in for their coffee and pastry on their way to work. By 9 a.m., however, it slowed down and the other regulars—the ones who were fond of gossiping—were entering the cafe, probably anxious to debate the latest murder.

As Nicole wiped down the counter following the onslaught of rush hour patrons, she eyed the Knitting for Good ladies who had just sat down at a table in the front corner. She wasn't sure how much knitting they were doing for charity lately. It actually seemed as if they were coming in beyond their typical weekly schedule more recently. There were some days they weren't knitting at all, in fact, meaning it had also become a social hangout. She also made the same observation about the Knights chess club. Nicole found that quite interesting and considered Susie's comment from the morning about how business had really picked up. Whatever they were doing right, Nicole hoped to keep it up.

Susie lightly touched Nicole's arm, rousing her

out of her thoughts, and said, "Go ahead, sweetie. I'll take the orders at the register while you wait on Knitting for Good." She winked.

Nicole smiled at Susie as she grabbed a notepad to take their orders and headed in the direction of Doris, Mary, and Charlotte. "Good morning, ladies, and Happy New Year! What can I get you this morning?"

"Nicole! I heard you saw another dead body!" said Charlotte, quite loudly. A few of the other patrons looked over as Nicole turned red. The typically quiet woman always seemed to say the most shocking things at the worst times.

"Yes, I was at the party—" started Nicole.

"How loud was that music? No one heard the gunshot? No one was around Phil Martini at the moment it happened? It's so hard to believe," said Doris. "Please, sit with us a moment. We don't even want to waste time ordering anything yet. We'll give you our orders when we're done with you."

Nicole's eyes grew wide, but she was hopeful these ladies might shed some light or give her another angle to explore, so she complied. "Okay...well, we were all up at the dance floor dancing right after midnight. When the band took a break, we were on our way back to our tables when we heard a woman scream. I later found out it was Don Martini's lady friend, Clarisa, who discovered the body." Nicole was about to tell the ladies that the murderer used a silencer on the gun when she suddenly had a fleeting memory of being at Don Martini's house, that he was the first person to indicate that the murderer used a silencer. But how would he know that? True, it made sense a silencer must have been used, since no one heard the shot. The music could have easily masked whatever remained of the sound, if any. But it made her wonder for a brief moment.

"Aha! What did I tell you, ladies. Marjorie ordered her husband dead and made sure Jeannette got her before the kill," said Mary.

Nicole was always amazed at how direct the old women could be at times!

"How did you know she wasn't there?" asked Nicole.

"Typical Marjorie. Doesn't like to get her hands dirty. I figured she wasn't the one who discovered the body because she wasn't there," said Mary. "It also confirms my suspicion that she wanted him dead. After all, there were rumors he was going to change his will."

"Really? How do you know?" Now Nicole was getting somewhere. More leads.

Doris spoke up. "I'm not supposed to know this, so let's keep this among us, ladies. I know I already told you ladies this morning but this fact bears repeating." She arched her eyebrows and leaned in closer to the table. "A close friend of mine works as an administrative assistant in the law office for the lawyer Phil Martini retains, Baylor and Baylor. She had to set up an appointment in Tom Baylor's calendar regarding a will update for Phil Martini."

"Oh my, the plot does thicken, doesn't it?" said Nicole. "What if she had her husband killed so that the will would remain the same?"

"Exactly. Most likely she will gain control of the hotel now and she can do what she wants with it, and who knows what other things she wants," added Doris.

Nicole pondered what Doris said. "But, how do we know she didn't kill her husband herself? And how do we know the will change would have been unfavorable?"

"As I said, she doesn't get her hands dirty. I know that woman well from attending many charity events," said Mary.

Charlotte nodded. "And, Al Roman had

become a new operations manager for Phil in the last year. Phil was getting up in years and wanted someone to help him with his businesses, someone privy to insider knowledge in case something happened to Phil. Rumor has it he was going to give Al a controlling share of his business upon his death." Charlotte's voice reduced to a whisper. "Not to mention that Marjorie didn't very much like Al. She didn't like him getting involved *at all*!"

"Interesting," was all Nicole could muster. Her brain was trying to process all the details she had gathered the past few days. From Don Martini talking about Jeannette Pierson and her husband to the Knitting for Good ladies talking about Marjorie trying to avoid a will change. It still begged the question for who actually committed the murder, too.

"That's a good start for Nicole, right, ladies?" asked Doris. The other two nodded.

"But I'm not supposed to be doing detective work. And you know Dean isn't supposed to intervene based on his contract," said Nicole.

"Dear, you have to learn to trust yourself. You have a knack for this murder stuff. While it may have seemed accidental in the past three murders, the bottom line is that you confronted the murderer in each case! That means you need to start honing your skills. And maybe take a self-defence class while you're at it," said Charlotte. Nicole was stunned to hear someone practically repeat what Lia had told her earlier that week. Solving murders was the last thing she expected to do when she decided to return to Rosewood.

"I appreciate the faith you have in me. Now what can I get you? asked Nicole. After she took down their orders for cappuccinos and macaroon cookies, she turned around and headed for the kitchen. On her way, she was intercepted by Don's friend, Max, who just walked in, with Clarisa by his side.

"Nicole, Max isn't doing well. He's so stressed out in the hospital. We just came from there." Max looked downcast and his voice sounded heavy.

"I'm so sorry to hear that, Max. I just visited him yesterday. I thought he was doing better?" Nicole looked in Clarisa's direction.

"Physically he's okay, I suppose, but emotional-ly...that's another story, Nicole," said Clarisa. Susie must have realized what was going on because she winked to Nicole, grabbed the notepad from her —as if to say that she would take care of the orders.

"Listen, can we sit down for a minute?" Max looked around nervously.

"Sure." Nicole gestured for them to sit at a table at the opposite corner of the cafe.

"I don't trust those Knitting ladies. I know they are saying it's Marjorie, but it's not. You have to believe Don! He knows more than them!" pleaded Max.

"Can you tell me why Don believes Jeannette broke in and that her husband killed Phil? I don't understand, and the police don't, either."

Max looked around the room again and then gestured for Nicole to move closer. He did the same with Clarisa. "Listen. I need you to promise me you will keep this between us. No telling Dean. You just can't. This is why Don couldn't tell you everything, but I'm afraid someone might try to kill Don off based on what he knows."

"Oh my goodness!" Nicole's heart skipped a beat. She had certainly developed a fondness for her old Mr. Martini and she didn't want anything to happen to him. "Okay, I promise. This is awkward, but I understand that confidentiality is required at times. I don't want anything to happen to Mr. Martini." She felt nervous saying this, but at the same time she wasn't sure what else to do.

"Listen, I understand from Clarisa that Don mentioned that Phil does a lot of deals. Well, one of the reasons the guy is so rich is because he is a well-known private financier." Max moved his head up and down emphatically. "Not to mention he deals in cash a lot, if you know what I mean. And Phil told Don last week that he felt people were taking advantage of him and he wanted his outstanding loans to be resolved. So he put some pressure on a few folks. One of whom, I am fairly certain, was Oliver Pierson. And that, my dear Nicole, is your murderer."

Nicole's jaw dropped. "But the break-in?"

"My theory is that Jeannette was already visiting her friend and that she took a moment to see if Phil had recorded the loan in any way." He shook his head. "But once Phil saw her in the office, he probably called the police just to scare her away."

"Ohh. Hmm, Dean did mention that they didn't see any signs of a break-in from the outside, so they weren't clear on how anyone broke into the house. They felt his claims for an attempted murder was unfounded."

"Yeah, he was just doing that to scare Jeannette off his property. I suspect she probably wanted to destroy any evidence of the loan, knowing what her husband was planning." Nicole saw Max look over in the direction of Knitting for Good. "Don't listen to the old ladies. They think they know it all, but we know the truth." He shook his head. "I don't know how you're going to pull it off, but somehow you need to engineer it so that Pierson is discovered to be the murderer. I just wish I could help you, but I can't think straight. I figured if we got our heads together, maybe we could prevent the next murder."

"Why do you think he'll go after Mr. Martini, I mean, Don?" asked Nicole.

"Because Don accidentally overheard a conversation in the next room when he was visiting Phil one time at the hotel. Oliver didn't know his brother was in the next room when he opened his big mouth. He was very upset when he realized Don was there." Clarisa's eyebrows furrowed as Max explained everything to Nicole.

"You're not going to believe this, but I'm actually going to the Pierson Gallery tonight with Dean. I'm assuming he'll be there," started Nicole.

Max raised his finger in the air. "Not a word to Dean." Nicole felt a knot in the pit of her stomach. She felt awkward purposely holding back a piece of information from Dean, but at the same time she didn't know what else to do. She made a promise and got herself into this mess.

"I know. I won't say anything, but I will keep my eyes and ears open. Maybe we can compare notes again tomorrow?" asked Nicole.

Max looked at Clarisa who nodded in return. "We'll come back tomorrow after we stop in the hospital again. Can we have two coffees and cannolis to go? I'm sure the cannolis will cheer Don up. We're heading back there now."

"Sure," smiled Nicole. "And thanks for the information. I'll do my best."

Nicole walked back to the kitchen, stupefied. Susie put her hand on her arm and said, "I don't want to know. But I won't be surprised if this town tears itself apart the next few days accusing one another of murder, while the real murderer sits back and laughs."

Susie's comment sent a chill through Nicole's body. She was probably right.

CHAPTER EIGHT

NICOLE'S HEAD was spinning as she tried to wrap her mind around all the details she became privy to in the morning. Those details opened up an even bigger can of worms in terms of open questions. While she was happy to get the insights, she started to feel that she was in over her head, especially with the agreement not to tell Dean about Phil Martini's loans. She assumed the loans were undocumented to the government so that he wouldn't get taxed on the interest he was collecting. That was probably why Max had hinted at cash transactions, hence the reason he didn't want law enforcement to know about it. But now Nicole was stuck between a rock and a hard place. She couldn't talk to Dean about it and that made her feel bad. She knew she couldn't bring it up to him, not only because she had promised Max, but also because it would put Dean in an unethical situation and he would have to report it. Her only option now was to try to solve the murder as quickly as possible to get the mess behind her.

In the meantime, she tried to focus on other things. She and Susie had decided on hiring someone, so she started drawing up an advertisement that she hoped to place in the paper. She worked on it late morning during the lull and set it aside when the lunch crowd came in for small bites and their afternoon cups of coffee.

When the cafe got slow after lunch, Nicole decided she needed to do something, something other than tell Dean. She desperately wanted to tell someone else so that she could sort all the information, but she was worried about violating her agreement with Max. He mentioned he wanted to keep it between them but then specifically banned Dean from knowing anything. But hadn't he said Don's life was at stake? What else could Nicole do if she wanted to keep Don alive but couldn't tell the police?

Nicole considered her options and thought about confiding in Lia. While Lia was an accountant, she didn't have the Martini family as clients, and that would mean she could be privy to the details without the obligation to report anything. Besides, all of the information Nicole got from Max was second-hand. If she shared that with Lia in confidence, she might be able to clear her head and plan her next course of action better. But telling Dean wouldn't be good because he'd had to investigate, and again there was the ethical dilemma.

But, she would still feel guilty if she told anyone, since she had made a promise after all. She closed her eyes and shook her head vigorously, frustrated that she didn't know what to do. She was starting to get a headache.

"A penny for your thoughts?" asked Susie.

"Funny, Lia said the same thing to me the other night." Nicole suddenly looked up at Susie and thought perhaps it was a little sign that she should confide in her friend after all. She needed help, and Don's life could be at stake. That was it, the decision was made.

"Anything I can help you with?" Susie asked. "It's slow in here now. Do you need to step out?"

"Actually, yes. I was thinking of filing that ad for the new hire at the Rosewood Gazette. Maybe I could use some fresh air, too. I'm going to step out for a while and I'll be back in a few hours so that you can go home. I'm going to close the cafe early today anyway since I'm also going to that art show. I don't believe the Knights will be playing tonight. Besides, they are probably all visiting Don in the hospital."

Susie smiled. "I think that's a wise decision. The temperatures are going to drop tonight anyway, so I doubt we'd get too many people. See you later, dear."

Nicole went to the back to fetch her bag and coat. She then dialed Lia's number.

"I've been waiting to hear from you all day! I didn't want to bother you, though. I figured it was a bear getting the cafe up and running again," said Lia.

"You know, you could answer the phone by saying hello, my friend," said Nicole in a light voice.

"You sound so tired. Are you okay?" asked Lia.

"I'm in over my head. I need to go over a few things with you, in the strictest confidence of course. I feel bad that I'm breaking someone else's confidence, but Don's life could be at stake! I need to make an exception here!"

"Oh, my! Where should I meet you?" asked Lia.

"I need to stop at the Rosewood Gazette first. Maybe I can meet you there and then we'll walk back to your office."

"Sounds good. See you in ten."

Nicole felt a little better now that she had a plan to not only hire more help, which she needed, but also map out the information about the murder with her friend. She moved her car to a municipal lot that was between the Rosewood Gazette and Lia's office, figuring it was a good place to park. As she walked towards the door of the newspaper, she spotted her friend.

"This will just take a minute." Lia nodded and they walked in together. When they reached the reception area, Nicole said, "Hi, I'm looking to place an ad in the paper. May I go ahead to the advertising desk for that?" Nicole looked behind the receptionist to refresh her memory about the open floor plan layout. She had been there when she first took over the cafe, but hadn't needed to advertise much since. And then she spotted the not-so-friendly reporter, Danielle Pruitt. Danielle had been unkind to Nicole around the time Stuart Helm had been murdered, though her disposition had improved slightly since she got a book deal. But there was one other nagging issue with her—she'd had an interest in Dean for some time, though Nicole heard she was dating someone now. She hoped that Dean was finally out of Danielle's head.

The receptionist stood up and turned her body to the left, raising her arm. "Yes, it's right over there. You can go there directly."

"Great, thanks." Nicole and Lia walked over to the desk where they were met with a friendly man, probably in his late 20s, wearing a funny combination of a baseball cap with a yellow sport jacket.

"Hi, Nicole. How can I help you today?" asked the young man.

"Oh, you remember me? I'd like to place an ad for a week. I'm looking for help in my cafe," said Nicole. Lia turned her body to give Nicole the slightest look. Nicole knew Lia was taking in his wardrobe choices.

The young man gave Nicole one of the biggest smiles she ever saw. She couldn't help but smile back, he just exuded radiance. She handed him the paper where she had written the ad. "Thank you. This looks great. We set up your account with us the last time, so we'll go ahead and bill you directly.

You should see the ad in the paper by tomorrow. Anything else I can help you with?"

"That's it! Thanks so much for your help!" said Nicole.

Still smiling quite broadly, the young man answered, "You're so welcome! Hope to see you again soon!"

As Nicole and Lia walked away, Lia said, "Wow, wish everyone in the world was that friendly! Well, I think he had a thing for you. Want to date a younger man? He's probably only about eight to ten years younger than you!"

Nicole elbowed her friend. "I'm taken, remember?" Suddenly, Danielle Pruitt was directly in their faces. "Oh, hello, Danielle."

"Hi," said Danielle with a very fake smile. "So, what do you know about the murder? I'm writing an article." Danielle looked a little different up close than Nicole remembered. Then it hit her, her hair was a little less spiky this time. Maybe she was growing it out, or letting it soften?

"I probably know just as much as you, Danielle," replied Nicole, careful to keep her tone even. As good-natured as Nicole tended to be, she still felt irked by Danielle's presence and was worried it would show.

"Ah, but I bet Dean didn't tell you the latest," taunted Danielle with a wink. "Winston James, the concierge at the hotel, came forward and said he overheard Don on the phone with his friend Max soon before midnight in the lobby, asking his friend to bring his gun to the hotel for him."

Nicole gasped. "That can't be right! He would never hurt his brother!"

Danielle, "Guess you're not so special to your man, huh? Why didn't he tell you? I'll tell you why. Because the whole town knows that you're trying to help Don." Danielle raised her head with an air of snobbery. "I thought engineers were objective and impartial. Guess that's why you couldn't cut it as an engineer and had to become a cafe owner. How ridiculous."

"Hey, wait a second!" Nicole's blood started to boil. Lia grabbed her friend's elbow, probably to caution her to calm down.

"Tsk. Tsk. So sensitive. Still don't get what Dean sees in you. Good day, ladies." Danielle promptly walked away.

"Let's get out of here," said Nicole. They quickly walked out the front door, not saying a word.

"Goodbye!" the receptionist faintly said. Nicole was so anxious to leave she didn't even turn around.

"The nerve of that woman!" said Nicole.

"She surely knows how to push your buttons." Lia faced her friend directly and put her hands on Nicole's shoulders. "Now the big question is, are you unknowingly protecting a murderer?"

CHAPTER NINE

LIA USHERED Nicole into her accounting practice around the corner from the Rosewood Gazette and then closed the door to her private office inside. "Here, sit down. I'll get you some water."

"It just can't be, Lia. But maybe Danielle is right...maybe I'm too biased. I just can't imagine the man who plays chess in my cafe every week killing his brother." Nicole closed her eyes and hung her head in despair. Lia placed the cup of water beside her.

"Okay, why don't you break down everything you know for me. Maybe we can figure this out together."

"But what about Dean? Do you think Danielle

was right? Maybe he didn't want to tell me." Nicole shook her head and then took a sip of water.

"Why don't you call him? See what he says. In worst case you tell him what Danielle said and see how he reacts." Lia shrugged. "What's the worst that can happen?"

"I don't want to put too much pressure on him, you know? Things are going well between us. We've been talking about a future. And if he feels pressured, he may become less interested."

"Ahh, maybe that's why you've been so reserved all along. So afraid of losing him?"

Nicole's eyes moistened. "Yes, I suppose that's part of it."

"Go ahead and call. I doubt he'll be upset with you. Just see what he says."

"Okay." Nicole took another sip of water and then took a deep breath. She dialed and he picked up right away.

"Hi Nicole, I'm glad you called. I didn't want to bother you earlier. I figured you and Susie were swamped! How's your first day back?" asked Dean. Nicole started to feel a little silly that she hadn't heard from Dean. Maybe he was simply being respectful of her time.

"A bit rough, but something good did happen

today. Susie and I agreed to hire help, actually. We both want a better work-life balance. I'll explain more about what triggered this later. So, anyway, I went with Lia to the Rosewood Gazette to place the ad for help and Danielle Pruitt confronted me." Nicole's voice started shaking so she paused.

"Oh, your best buddy, huh?" He laughed. "I'm sure she laid it on thick about Don calling Max for his gun." Nicole practically jumped out of her chair. She looked over at Lia who gave her quizzical look.

"Yes! That's exactly what she said!" exclaimed Nicole.

"I'm sorry you got blindsided there. She was snooping around in the police department right when we had taken Max in for questioning. Winston James from the hotel was still at the station when she arrived and he went and told her."

"Why didn't Winston mention this the other night?" asked Nicole.

"Actually, he was already gone when the murder happened. There was an overnight manager and we did talk to him, but Winston had gone home for the night when his shift ended at midnight. He didn't report it when he heard the conversation because he thought Don was joking. He said Don didn't sound very angry on the phone but almost matter-of-fact, so he thought it was a weird attempt at humor," said Dean. "But, who knows? We have to take it seriously now. It doesn't help that records show a gun is registered to Don, which we actually can't find now. And we had people check Don's house and Max's. The gun is nowhere to be seen. Plus, the murder weapon is still missing. Are they one and the same? Perhaps."

Nicole's thoughts were racing. It wasn't looking good for her dear Mr. Martini. "What about the silencer? Is that registered?" asked Nicole. Suddenly a chill went down her spine as she recalled that little detail Don had mentioned at his house, that he knew the murder weapon had a silencer.

"We're assuming there was a silencer, yes, since no one heard the shot. But technically they're not legal in New Jersey. They are legal in other states, however. Someone could always get it illegally, though, or through a friend in another state. I honestly don't think it's that hard to obtain." Now Nicole was really getting an education! But what did it matter, anyway? Her friend Don was a suspect and now it sounded like Max could have been an accomplice. Now she was really in a fix. Should she tell Dean what Max told her in the morning at the cafe? Maybe he was baiting her, hoping she would tell Dean so that it would take the suspicion off Don and Max after all. Nicole was starting to panic at the web that was being weaved around her. Maybe Susie was right about the town tearing itself apart with all the accusations, and she the one getting wrapped into it.

"I'm learning a lot. Thanks for explaining all that," Nicole's voice faded. She was worried about the men whom she regarded as friends. And the guilt she felt from withholding information from Dean wasn't helping.

"I've got to get back and help the chief with a burglary case he's been trying to crack. Are we still on for tonight? I'll pick you up around 6:50 pm." Nicole looked over at Lia who was sitting at her desk doing paperwork, probably killing time while she waited for Nicole to get off the phone.

"Yes, I'm looking forward to it. See you then. Bye now."

"Bye!" Nicole heard Dean hang up.

"So it's not looking good for your Don, huh?" asked Lia.

Nicole spotted the wooden doors encasing a whiteboard on the wall. She gestured to it and said, "May I?"

"Sure, go ahead. Here are some markers."

Nicole blew out a breath, gathering her thoughts, as she opened the doors to the whiteboard. "Okay, so let me list out everything in bullet points in chronological order from what I've been told, but this needs to stay between us. Jeannette Pierson picked up Marjorie from the hotel at 11 p.m. Don had an argument with his brother and left the room before midnight. He had a phone conversation with Max, heard by Winston James, and told him to bring his gun to the hotel. Clarisa said she left both Don and Phil at the table after midnight to dance, so maybe he returned to the table briefly before going to the bathroom?" Nicole sat down, looking at the board. Lia just stared at it. "But now I have to give you the behind the scenes information that was privately shared with me this morning by several cafe regulars."

"Okay?" Lia cocked her head.

"The Knitting for Good ladies told me that Phil Martini had an appointment set with his lawyer to change his will. Apparently he's got this new operations manager Al Roman, whom Marjorie does not like, and it's rumored he was going to leave Al a significant portion of his business to him." Nicole took a breath. "And Max and Clarisa visited me this morning, too, to tell me that Phil often had, let's just say, interesting loan agreements with people and Oliver Pierson was one of them. Phil was putting pressure on those who had loans with him to pay up. And they think Jeannette tried to destroy any evidence of the loan at Phil's house the other night, with Oliver actually committing the murder in the ballroom."

"Wow." Lia's eyes were wide. "That's a lot to take in. This is certainly a complicated one!" Lia stood up and got herself a cup of water. She looked at the board while she sipped her water and then sat back down, facing Nicole. "So, what's your next step?"

"I'll visit the art show with Dean tonight and see if anything is up with Oliver Pierson and possibly Marjorie if she's there with Oliver's wife, Jeannette." Nicole shook her head. "That's the part I don't get. Would Jeannette and her husband plot to kill her friend's husband?"

"Well, maybe his death was a win for all of them. Getting out of the loan and keeping the will to Marjorie's taste," replied Lia.

"I know, but that would still mean less money for Marjorie if Oliver didn't repay the loan completely. Or maybe she was willing to modify the terms of the loan, to give her friend's husband more time." Nicole rubbed her chin.

"Good point. Okay, so what happens after the art show?"

Nicole brushed her sweater with her hand, thinking. "I was thinking of calling my cousin, Tony, to see if he could connect us with an estate lawyer, maybe someone who could explain what happens if a husband changes his will in New Jersey. I thought that the wife still gets a significant share regardless, but I'm not a lawyer."

"That's an interesting point. It might at least rule out Marjorie, but at the same time we don't know if Marjorie herself committed the murder or someone she hired. If it was someone she hired, who? Although it could have been her friends as we just said." Lia bit her lip. "But, if Marjorie doesn't know law well enough, she could have been driven to think she'd lose his estate when in reality, she could have still claimed some of it most likely."

"I got the sense from the Knitting for Good ladies that she's the type of person who wants everything, and she doesn't get her hands dirty." Nicole raised her eyebrows.

"Aha. Definitely worth exploring with a lawyer then. What else?" asked Lia.

"I think I want to stay away from the Don and Max thing now. I'm not sure what to think there at the moment. Nothing more to explore. Would rather eliminate these other possibilities and narrow it down until things become a bit clearer about Don," said Nicole. "But, I do think it might be valuable to go back to the scene of the crime at some point, so I will try to do that in the next few days, too."

"Okay, so why don't you go to the art show tonight, and set up an appointment with the lawyer for tomorrow? I can join you for the lawyer meeting if you'd like," offered Lia.

"Yes, I would appreciate the company. Okay, we'd better erase this so no one sees it," said Nicole, gesturing to the whiteboard. "And I have to get going if I want to close up the cafe and fix myself up for tonight." Nicole exhaled a breath of relief. "Thanks for this, Lia. I'm starting to feel a little better now. I had so much information swimming in my head before, and I was overwhelmed with all the suggestions I received today."

"Good! You'll be in a better head space for your date with Dean tonight. Speaking of which, what are you wearing? That little black dress you got from Tess's Boutique when we shopped there again after Christmas?" asked Lia.

"You bet!" said Nicole with a smile. She was definitely looking forward to her date. And she was looking forward to getting more information about the Piersons, too.

CHAPTER TEN

NICOLE LOOKED out the window of Dean's car and admired the holiday decorations that were still adorning the streets of Rosewood. From lit wreaths on the lamps, to a beautiful Christmas tree display in front of the town hall, the holiday spirits were still in full bloom after Christmas.

"You know, I haven't actually visited the art gallery since I returned to Rosewood a few years ago. Maybe this art thing isn't going to work out so well. You'd think I would have visited already." Dean laughed.

"Well, now we get to check it out together. Besides, I'm not really sure how it works. It seems like one of those exclusive things. I never see anyone visiting the gallery if there isn't a special collection or event being advertised." Nicole thought more about how the Piersons owned the gallery and tried to remember any details she had heard about the gallery over the past year. The only thing she could recall was that the husband, Oliver, seemed to oversee it. But that thought revealed a distant memory from when she first took over the cafe. She vaguely remembered the Knitting for Good ladies talking about how the gallery was supposed to close at one point. But the following week the paper featured a "grand reopening" ad about an event hosting a famous painter. Nicole realized Oliver probably got to reopen his gallery with funding from Phil after all. Now things were starting to come together for her, and just in time for the event that evening. Maybe Max was onto something about Oliver secretly getting a loan from Phil!

As Dean drove through the streets of Rosewood, Nicole continued to consider the loan angle. At least it was the angle that made her feel the most comfortable. The only problem was, how to prove it, not to mention the fact that she had to keep it a secret from Dean. Now *that* was eating away at her.

"Thanks for being so supportive about my interest in art. I do find it very therapeutic. I drew a lot as a kid and sort of stopped when I was in the FBI. But after Jane...I picked it up again to help me cope," Dean looked across to Nicole at a red light.

Nicole returned his smile. "I think it's very healthy."

"But what about you? I don't really know what your hobbies are?" asked Dean.

"That's a good question. To be honest, I never really gave it much thought. But if I consider what I do when I'm not baking, running the cafe or teaching classes, then it would be reading and writing."

"Writing? Oh, right. You said something about a novel when Stuart Helm was murdered and Detective Dawkins confiscated your computer. He didn't wipe out the novel, did he?"

"I still have it, and I poke at it here and there." Nicole chuckled. "Not sure when I'll ever finish it."

"May I ask what it's about?" asked Dean. Nicole noticed they were in front of the gallery now. Before Nicole could answer, he said, "We're going to have to find a spot on the street. Their tiny lot is full already!" Nicole thought she might be able to get out of telling him about the topic of her novel, but he looked over again and said, "You don't have to tell me if you're not comfortable."

"You're not going to like it. It's a murder mystery."

And with that, Dean burst out laughing. "Uh huh! Well, you certainly have had enough experience in that department to write a good story." Dean opened his door and said, "Don't move, I'll come around to help you out." He moved around the car quickly and opened the door for her. Nicole stepped out in high heels with a dressy coat over her little black dress. He gave her a quick kiss on the lips and then said, "Beautiful, as always. Come on, let's go inside." He took Nicole's arm and led her down the sidewalk and into the foyer of the gallery. As they walked in, Nicole spotted the coat check. "May I?" Dean helped Nicole remove her coat. He handed their coats to the attendant and took the ticket from her.

Nicole noticed Dean was wearing a striking, three-piece pinstripe suit. Dean caught her admiring his suit and she felt sheepish. "Very handsome. Is that a new suit?" asked Nicole.

"Yes, in fact, it is. I took advantage of some of the post-holiday deals and decided to update my wardrobe a bit. Besides, I have big plans for wining and dining you this year." Dean's comment made Nicole blush, and she didn't know what to say. Then a server passed them and offered them sparkling wine, which they accepted.

Nicole watched Dean as he sipped his drink and his eyes shifted around the room. "This is quite good. Oh, I recognize the instructor for my art class. He looks just like his picture. Maybe we can go meet him?" said Dean.

"Sounds good!" They carefully made their way through the crowd. Nicole didn't recognize anyone from Rosewood at first. She assumed the attendees must have been from some of the more elite towns surrounding them, such as West Branford, where most of the residents commuted into New York City. Then, she happened to catch a view of Oliver in a corner with his wife, Jeannette, and Marjorie. Marjorie didn't look the slightest bit upset that her husband was dead. Marjorie must have noticed Nicole, too, because she suddenly looked intensely at her, and it gave Nicole a chill.

"Hello, Professor Corbett, I'm Dean Coogan, and this is my date, Dr. Nicole Capula. I'm going to be in your Intro to Oil and Acrylic Painting class this semester."

"It's nice to meet you. So glad you met the first requirement, attending this event! I must admit I have an ulterior motive, though. One of my pieces is being displayed this evening. It's right over there."

"Wow, the couple dancing in the rain? It's beautiful!" remarked Nicole.

"Do you have a Ph.D. in art? I heard Dean refer to you as a doctor?" asked the short man with salt-and-pepper hair, perhaps mid 50s. He wore a brown tweed suit. Nicole surmised that this was how an artist should look, though she hadn't come across many artists in her life.

"No, no, in chemical engineering, actually. I used to work in the chemical industry, but I inherited the Cannoli Cafe in town so that's my main focus now. I do teach courses part-time at the University of New Jersey, though."

"Oh, impressive! Well, Dean, it was nice to meet you and especially Nicole, if I may say so! You have good taste, so I'll be expecting great things from you!"

Dean laughed. "It's great meeting you. Congratulations on the exhibit!"

Just then, Oliver came over to talk to Professor Corbett while Jeannette took Dean's arm, mumbling something about needing to talk with him, while Marjorie grabbed Nicole and said, "Come on, I'll show you the ladies' room." Nicole looked back at Dean but Jeannette had managed to corral him in such a way that a lot of attendees were surrounding him. She decided to comply with Marjorie's wishes, not wanting to make a scene, but she was concerned that she was going straight into the lion's den.

Marjorie opened the door of the luxurious women's room and pushed Nicole against the wall. No one else was inside. She grabbed Nicole's arms and said, "Stop causing trouble for my friends, Jeannette and her husband. I know Max and Clarisa talked to you this morning. I saw it through the window of your cafe, and I imagine it's all over the loan my husband took. Stay out of this and let the police do their job. Don is guilty. He deserves to be locked up, or even worse. And if you don't stay out of this, you might get caught in the crossfire, too." Marjorie's steel blue eyes were intensely focused on Nicole's. Nicole couldn't help but shake in fear. She was absolutely in over her head, and the worst part was that she wouldn't be able to tell Dean about it. "And I know what that pretty little head of yours is thinking. But you know you can't tell your boyfriend, because then

Don's life will be in danger. I can promise you that!"

Nicole just stared forward in disbelief, nodding. "I understand."

"Good. Enjoy the exhibit." And with that, Marjorie left Nicole in the women's room. Feeling very rattled, she walked over to the sinks and mirror. She didn't want to mess up her makeup by splashing water on her face, so she just stood there at first, trying to catch her breath. She at least wanted to wash her hands. She felt so dirty after the confrontation with Marjorie. That triggered a memory of when she studied *Macbeth* in high school and it made her shudder. She certainly didn't want any blood on her hands, metaphorically speaking. Or physically.

Now she felt quite strongly that Marjorie, Jeannette and her husband were all in on Phil's murder. They were thick as thieves that night, and it seemed they purposely broke up Dean and Nicole. It didn't make sense that Don's life would be in danger unless he knew something he shouldn't, which was absolutely the case. She shuddered at the thought of Oliver Pierson being the one who killed Phil. She was within just a few feet of him earlier, and she would probably be a few feet away from him again momentarily.

After washing and drying her hands, she realized she needed to get back to the exhibition regardless. She walked out of the women's room and looked around. The bathroom was located on the edge of the gallery. She could return to the party where everyone else was, or she could wander through the hallway for a moment and see if she could pick up any other clues about Oliver. She decided on the latter, though she gave herself a time limit since Dean was waiting. As she went down the hallway, she felt a breeze. *That's odd*, she thought. She continued down the passage, noticing it was getting colder and colder, to find the back door open. She stepped out into the freezing cold and was stunned to see a figure running away from the building. She nearly followed the person, but it was too cold and she was in heels. She wouldn't have gotten far. She tried to make out if it was a man or woman but she couldn't tell; it was too dark out and there were hardly any lights in the area where the figure was running. She turned around to walk back inside when she heard a loud scream coming from the gallery. *Oh no, not again*, she thought.

Nicole raced back to the gallery to find a swarm

of people looking up at the second floor balcony, blood dripping onto the first floor. Dean raced up the stairs. Everyone stood in silence as they waited for the verdict. "Oliver Pierson is dead. Nobody move!"

CHAPTER ELEVEN

Nicole and Lia sat at the kitchen table, drinking their coffee and eating scrambled eggs and toast. "Thanks so much for making breakfast for me. Last night was horrendous."

"I can't believe there was a second murder! See, isn't it good I stayed over after all? It's not safe right now!" said Lia. Ringo crept over to her. She smiled down at him and rubbed his head. "Plus, Ringo loves Aunt Lia! Don't you, Ringo?"

Nicole stayed silent, thinking about what happened last night, analyzing all the possibilities. The big questions were who, and why. The one thing she did know, however, was that last night's murder was carefully planned and executed. There had to be a reason behind it, and it was somehow connected to Phil Martini's murder. It was just too coincidental.

"Do you think you could at least stay home and rest this morning?" asked Lia.

"No, I don't think so." Nicole shook her head. "Susie is managing the cafe this morning, thank goodness, but I do need to go in soon since Max and Clarisa are expecting me based on our conversation yesterday morning." Nicole took another forkful of her eggs.

"So what are you going to tell them?" asked Lia as she held her mug in her hands.

"The truth. I mean, what can they expect after the police found a torn paper with blood on it—inside Oliver's jacket —with the words *Oliver Pierson: $1 million outstanding* written on it!" On the one hand, Nicole was relieved. She didn't have to tell Dean about the Oliver Pierson loan as if it was new information. So when he told her about the paper that was found, she explained that Max and Clarisa had told her about Phil Martini's private loans in confidence and that it put her in an awkward position given the fact that he is a private investigator, helping the police department at times. She also pointed out that Dean had informed her that Don's gun was missing the previous day, and she wasn't sure if she was being "played" by Don's friends to protect him. It was possible they were trying to get the police department to focus on Oliver Pierson to take the focus off of Don.

But that didn't take her profound feeling of guilt away.

"And how did Dean take your omission?" asked Lia.

"Much better than I expected." Nicole let out a sigh of relief. "He told me it's common for stuff like that to happen once an investigation starts. People like to point the finger at each other, and they will gossip and throw out lots of different information in the surrounding community without any substantiation, which was the case until last night. In the end, the proper investigation needs to unfold with clear evidence or first-hand accounts at least. And it was up to Don to share the truth about his brother and what he had witnessed."

"So he wasn't mad at you?" Lia wrinkled her forehead.

"Perhaps a little...It was hard to tell. Honestly, he seemed more concerned about the fact that Marjorie had cornered and threatened me in the bathroom." Nicole looked up at her friend, her eyebrows arched. "But I am a little worried about our relationship. I hope I didn't blow it."

"What? What are you talking about?" asked Lia. She was leaning on the edge of her seat.

"Marjorie pulled me into the ladies' room, pushed me against the wall, and held my arms while she told me to stay out of the investigation. She said Don would get hurt if I interfered. And she told me not to tell Dean, but given everything that happened last night I decided it was best to be open with him. He assured me that in light of what she said to me, the police will guard Don until they investigate her."

"Wow! Are you okay?" asked Lia. "Here, let me get you more coffee." Lia went ahead and filled a second cup for her friend. "Oh my goodness! This is unbelievable."

Nicole shuddered. "Thanks. I'm just a little shaken, that's all. It all happened so quickly. The other weird thing is, which I *did* tell Dean about, too, is that after I left the bathroom, I saw the back door was open to the building. I looked out and saw a figure running away, and just then I heard the scream.

"Ohh, interesting. So perhaps that was the murderer running away?" asked Lia.

Nicole nodded. "Most likely. It would make sense, at least."

"And where was your dear Marjorie when the body was found?" asked Lia. She shook her head.

"Gone. She had told someone she felt ill in the bathroom and said she was going out for fresh air and possibly wouldn't return." Nicole shook her head. "Convenient, huh? And you know the other weird part? Don Martini was released from the hospital yesterday afternoon, too."

"So what do you think?" asked Lia. Ringo decided to lie down on the floor next to Lia's feet.

Nicole stood up and started to pace in her kitchen. "I can't get that torn paper out of my mind. I think there had to be at least one other name on that loan record, possibly more." Nicole paused.

"So that could mean—"

"Maybe the killer wanted to expose the fact that Phil Martini financed those loans. Maybe that was the whole purpose of killing Oliver, just to put attention on it. That would make the investigation so wide the police wouldn't have a chance of finding him or her."

"Right, how would they even know where to

look? Phil Martini did business with tons of people and knew everybody," added Lia.

Nicole waved her finger in the air. "So the killer was clever. That person most likely broke into the office to retrieve the loan document, killed Phil so they wouldn't have to repay him, and then they essentially framed the murder of Phil Martini by pointing out the loan Oliver had, implying others with outstanding loans could have had motive to kill Phil."

"Or, maybe that was all a ruse on Marjorie's part to get the attention off of her," added Lia. "And I hate to say it, but it being a ruse on Don's part is possible, too. After all, he might have had a loan from his brother."

"The killer was clever. They set it up so that it could be practically anyone." Nicole shuddered after uttering that sentence.

"Did you ask Dean if they were getting finger-prints on the paper?" asked Lia.

"I did, and he said the problem is that if the killer at the party was smart enough, they might have handed Phil the paper to confuse him and then taken the shot. That way the paper would look legitimate if his prints came up. But they will check regardless."

Lia's eyes widened. "Whoa, not sure I would have thought of that! Guess that's why he was in the FBI. The force should really just put him on these cases officially. I think it's inefficient that they don't. He's always walking on eggshells trying not to overstep."

"I think they have some sort of rules about that since he's not actually an employee, but they could let him at least consult more. A discussion for another time! Anyway, I'm going to get ready to meet with Max and Clarisa now. Not much else we can do until I meet with them and that lawyer later." Nicole pressed her lips together, thinking. "Would you believe that Dean is actually endorsing our visit to the lawyer since Marjorie is now a suspect after her threats? He said they could use the information about how wills work!"

"When is the meeting?" asked Lia.

"Tony sent me an email confirming that we can meet the lawyer in West Branford this afternoon at 2 p.m."

"Great! That works out perfectly because I'm meeting a client over lunch in that area. Text me the address and I'll meet you there."

"Okay. I hope we get somewhere today. And I hope Oliver's murder was the last one connected to this case." Nicole closed her eyes. "What if we're dealing with a serial killer? What if we're dealing with something much, much bigger than we anticipated?"

And with that, she walked down the hall to get ready. It was going to be a rough day.

CHAPTER TWELVE

AFTER SHOWERING and putting on a fitted black pantsuit, Nicole stopped in the Cannoli Cafe, expecting to meet with Don and Clarisa. She felt a bit nervous about the meeting, especially since she was going to be honest about how she did not want to be pressured to omit things from Dean going forward. Things were going so well in their relationship lately. He was expressing himself more and seeming much more confident; she didn't want to ruin their new rhythm. But she was still worried he might have been disappointed in her for not immediately sharing some of the details she had heard the previous morning.

Nicole parked her car in the lot and walked in

the back door. After putting her coat and bag down, she passed through the kitchen to get to the front counter and noticed Susie manning the register. She turned around and gave Nicole a broad smile. "Hi, Nicole! Wow, don't you look fancy! What's the occasion?"

Nicole kept her voice at a low tone, not wanting to attract too much attention. "I'm actually meeting with a lawyer this afternoon. To ask details about this case. I can't say too much more on that. Speaking of which, have any of the regulars arrived like Max or the Knitting for Good ladies?" Nicole looked around the busy cafe. "Wow, a lot of people today."

"Yes, they're all gossiping about the murder at the art gallery. I hope you weren't still there when it happened! By the way, I think Doris and Charlotte are still here—over there in the corner."

"Oh yes, I see them." Nicole put her hand on Susie's arm. "I can't tell you how drained I am from all this! I definitely need to rest at home when all this is over. The sooner we can hire someone, the better!"

"Well, I have some news that might cheer you up! There is a woman over there...I believe her name is Celeste." Susie pointed with her pinky finger in the woman's direction. "She came in earlier saying she saw the ad and wants the job. Maybe you can go talk to her. I spoke with her for a while and I think she might be a good fit."

"Okay, I'll do that before I get involved with Knitting for Good!" Nicole chuckled as she approached the table-for-one where Celeste was sitting. "Hi, I'm Nicole, the owner of the Cannoli Cafe. I understand you're interested in working here?"

"Oh, yes, Nicole! It's so great to see you again!" said Celeste.

"Again?" asked Nicole, eyebrows furrowed.

"Oh, yes! I saw you dancing with that handsome man at the New Year's Eve party! We were sitting in the back, maybe that's why you didn't see us. You see, my husband works in the city with Tony, and he invited us. In fact, that's why I'm interested in the job. Larry doesn't come home until 8 p.m. and I haven't worked in years, since I stayed home to raise my kids. Well, the kids are all grown up and I'm home alone all the time! I figured I could clean the house, cook dinner ahead of time, and then come out here every afternoon to work for you. When I get home, I can just warm up our meal. It would be so much better than being home alone all the time, let me tell you!" Nicole found Celeste's story interesting. She certainly came across as friendly and articulate and would probably be good for handling the customers in the front. She also seemed to have the same spirit as Aunt Lucia, and that could never be a bad thing!

"Would you like to work this week on a trial basis? If we're both pleased with how it works out, you can stay on after. If you come in at 1 p.m. and close up at 7 p.m. during the week, that would work out great." Nicole was liking this idea more and more. This was going to give both Nicole and Susie more freedom, as long as the trial worked out. Celeste would just need some training during the first week, of course. "When can you start?"

"Today? I can watch Susie in action and maybe help her out after I get the hang of it."

"That sounds good to me! You have yourself a deal!" The women smiled at each other and shook hands. Nicole turned around and gave a thumbs-up sign to Susie at the register, who also looked pleased.

She bid Celeste a good day and then moved on

to Doris and Charlotte in the corner. "Hello, ladies. Is Mary okay?" asked Nicole.

"Oh yes, she had a pottery class this morning. She tried to get us to join her, but we don't like getting dirty, you know!" answered Doris.

Charlotte piped up, "Speaking of which, we heard the police are onto Marjorie after all."

"She threatened me. It was very upsetting," Nicole grimaced.

"We heard. The nerve of that woman!" said Doris.

"She's a slippery one. You'd better watch out for her, you know," added Charlotte.

"Actually, I'm meeting a lawyer this afternoon to understand more about how wills work. Is there anything else you can think of that I should mention to him?" asked Nicole.

"I'm not sure what you can ask him about, dear. But have you considered that Jeannette and Marjorie are best friends, and they both lost their husbands to murder within a few days of each other? I would start looking into Jeannette's story, too," said Doris. Nicole's head was spinning. The previous murders seemed to have more clear-cut suspects. This one was a doozy, for sure.

"That's a good point. Thanks, ladies." Nicole looked around the cafe and realized it was late morning already. The lull had set it, and there was no Max or Clarisa in sight.

"Very interesting," she said to herself.

CHAPTER THIRTEEN

NICOLE DROVE through the hills of West Branford in a daze. Images of Don, Max and Clarisa in the cafe, the blood in the gallery, Oliver Pierson, Phil Martini, Marjorie in the bathroom, and even Jeannette Pierson cycled through her mind's eye. At a red light, she let her head fall back onto the headrest in the car. "Why am I even worrying about this anymore? It's the job of the police," she said to herself.

The light turned green. *Because Mr. Don Martini asked me to, that's why*, she thought. She tried to let her mind relax and went back to the beginning of all this. New Year's Eve. The Rosewood Hotel. He went through the trouble of introducing her to Clarisa. He was happy. Though he briefly mentioned being upset with his brother, he must have been happy overall, since he made the effort to walk over to her table, which was closer to the front of the room, not near the back where he was sitting. *This is a man who used to shout at me for his spaghetti.* But now he was more of a gentleman. At first she thought it was because they grew more comfortable with one another. There was a routine. He came in, she served him small bowls of spaghetti or macaroni if he was hungry, which he usually was, followed by cannolis. But it was more than that. It must have been this relationship with Clarisa. He must have seen glimpses of a happy future in his mind. His Knights routine, combined with companionship at his age, must have been the unique combination of forces he needed to show his softer, more gentleman-like personality that was hiding on the inside.

And what about what he said, about how he'd rather be arguing with his brother than have him gone? Now that she could believe. Even the Mr. Don Martini of before enjoyed a great argument. Even the old, grumpy Don wouldn't want a fly to hurt his brother, or someone to take away his precious debate partner. But someone did take away his brother. Who? Nicole felt more resolved than ever that it was not Don, despite "evidence" to the contrary. Did this Winston James, a supposed concierge, really overhear Don ask Max to bring his gun? Nicole stopped at another red light and then the lightbulb went off. Even if Don asked him that, which he wouldn't have, there's no way Max would have complied. No way. It just wouldn't make sense. Max was always the sensible one, getting Don to calm down, right from when Nicole first met the dynamic chess duo.

She exhaled a breath, feeling relieved. She at least decided that she discounted Don as a suspect (and any help on Max's part). She was following her gut on this one. And since she would have to pass the Rosewood Hotel on her way back from the lawyer, she was ready to meet that Winston James and dig a little more into his story. Maybe he had an ulterior motive for lying. After all, he worked for Phil Martini directly. Did anyone consider that he could have another agenda? Not to mention the fact that he would know the ins and outs of that hotel. It would be much easier for someone who knows the layout and security system (which apparently there is none) to pull off the murder. And that was another point. Most people would assume there are cameras in hotels. Who else would dare to bring a gun in and take a shot but someone who might know there are no cameras? Perhaps someone who works there.

Nicole was starting to feel better. Now she was getting somewhere. Maybe Susie was right—the whole town was pointing fingers at one another, or at least that small circle of Marjorie, Jeannette, Don, the Piersons, etc., but she was overlooking anyone who worked for him directly, particularly at the hotel. Now she had more she could explore, outside of all the gossip, that might really lead her somewhere. She actually smiled.

She overheard her phone GPS voice chirp, saying, "Destination will be on the right."

She knew Lia was out and about meeting some new clients in the West Branford area. *Good for her,* she thought. Her accounting business was going well. As she pulled into the lot for an office building, she spotted her friend's car on the other side. After parking a few spaces away, she took a breath, smoothed her clothes, and got out of the car.

"Fancy meeting you here, friend," said Lia.

Nicole smiled. "Thanks for meeting me here."

"Hmm, something's different. You almost seem happy," said Lia.

Nicole walked over to her friend and said," I

finally got some clarity when I was alone in my car. It's definitely not Don. Do you have plans after this? Maybe we can grab a drink at the hotel. I want to meet a certain Winston James."

"For a few minutes. I have another meeting at 4:30 pm in this area so I wouldn't be able to stay long, but I might be able to stop by for a bit."

"Okay. Well, let's see what we find out from Mr. Drew Blackburn, Esquire." The ladies walked into the office building and looked for the third floor, where his law practice was located. When they got on the elevator, Nicole noticed that Lia had dressed in a navy skirt suit that was peeking out through her open coat. Nicole knew she tended to dress up for outside client meetings, but Lia often looked quite fashionable and put-together no matter what she was wearing, even if she was not wearing business clothes.

When they exited the elevator, they saw a sign on the wall indicating a right arrow for office 302. "Here we go," said Nicole. They proceeded down the hall a few steps and opened the heavy door to go inside. They were met with a receptionist wearing tortoiseshell framed-glasses at a small reception area. "Hello, we have a 2 p.m. appointment with Mr. Blackburn. Dr. Nicole Capula and Ms. Lia Gibbiano."

"Gibbiano? Your last name is Gibbiano?" A handsome man with light brown hair and a trim black suit, perhaps in his late 30s, walked out of an office and approached Nicole and Lia. Lia glanced at Nicole, probably confused, since the appointment was really made through Nicole's cousin to meet with Nicole. Lia was simply going along for the ride.

"Yes, it is. Why?" Lia looked up at the man. Nicole found the encounter quite interesting to watch. She wasn't used to her friend coming across off-guard, but Lia did seem thrown off a bit.

"Please, come inside." Mr. Blackburn gestured for Nicole and Lia to sit in the red leather chairs opposite his desk. "I didn't realize you'd be coming today."

"I'm sorry, my cousin Tony Capula said we had a meeting for 2 p.m. with you. We just have a few questions about wills," said Nicole, her forehead wrinkled. She was starting to get nervous. This lawyer meeting was starting out very strangely.

"That's not what I mean." Mr. Blackburn looked over at Lia, a pained expression marking his face. "I had been thinking of contacting you about something, but I was trying to gather more evidence first."

"I'm sorry. You must have me mistaken with another client. I typically deal with the IRS directly on issues, not lawyers," said Lia, eyebrows arched.

"This is something...personal." The man closed his eyes, continuing to look pained. Nicole and Lia glanced at each other, very confused. "Please call me Drew. Because this is just the beginning."

Lia's mouth opened and she shook her head. "The beginning of what?" Her tone started to sound exasperated.

"The beginning of finding out what really happened to your parents." He looked up and stared directly into Lia's eyes.

"What?" Nicole saw her friend grow white. She put out her hand and touched her arm.

"You see, my father passed away a few months ago. And on his deathbed, he told me he has been plagued these past twelve years by the Gibby case."

"The Gibby case?" asked Lia.

"Yes. My father worked for the CIA. Your father worked as a government contractor, for an outside company doing scientific work. Your father had made a discovery about something at the top secret level. And then he was killed."

"No, my father and mother were killed in an auto accident." Lia was shaking her head profusely. Tears started to form in her eyes.

"The auto incident occurred later. We think your father and mother were killed first. Then they were placed in the vehicle, which was then rammed by a giant truck and caught, or put, on fire. To destroy all possible evidence. All while you were in Europe, thankfully away from all that." Mr. Blackburn looked almost relieved after he explained this to Lia. His shoulders became less rigid and he leaned back slightly. "I'm sorry, it's a lot to take in. But it was my father's dying wish to figure out what happened there. He knew you were an only child and that their deaths would be devastating to you. He also believed your mother may have known about the secret, and even if she didn't, apparently the party who killed them didn't want to take any chances...I'm so sorry." Drew moved a box of tissues across the desk. Nicole was quite sure that Lia was absolutely stunned. She put her arm around her friend who was quietly sobbing.

"Do you have any idea who did it?" asked Lia, between sobs.

"I have a few leads I'd like to go over with you at some point. But right now we don't really know. I would like to ask you to think about old conversations you had with your father. He may have told you in code at some point. In fact, I suspect he knew what was going to happen. Did he encourage you to go to Europe?" asked Drew.

Lia looked at Drew Blackburn with her mouth open. "Yes, and I was surprised at first, because they wanted me to stay local for my undergrad degree. Yet my dad was the one who told me to go abroad, saying it was a once-in-a-lifetime opportunity. It was definitely uncharacteristic for my parents."

"They were protecting you, Ms. Gibbiano." Drew Blackburn stared across into Lia's eyes. Meanwhile, Nicole sat there in disbelief, witnessing the exchange.

"You said Gibby before?" asked Lia.

"Yes, that was the name people referred to it internally. Sort of a code. Short for your last name, of course."

"May I go to the ladies' room? I need a moment," Lia looked over at her friend and nodded. Nicole nodded back. She knew that meant for Nicole to carry out what she needed to in her absence.

"Of course," said Drew.

After Lia exited the office, Nicole started, "I'm surprised you told her all that with me present."

"I know you're a close friend to her, almost like a sister. It was in the file."

Nicole's eyes widened. Her name was in a government document?

"Don't worry, this is all between us. I'm a lawyer and I'm trained to keep secrets. So was my dad, prior to his passing." Drew looked down. Clearly he was close to his dad. "Anyway, how can I help you today?"

Nicole took in a breath. She felt thrown off, too. She knew Lia's parents, the nicest people in the world. She felt a little rattled but realized she needed to stay focused and strong for her friend and to help solve the current case at hand. "Between us, of course. I was threatened the other night by Marjorie Martini, the wife of Phil Martini. My question is: could she have murdered Phil Martini if she feared that he was going to change his will?"

"Ahh, I heard you were something of a sleuth. And a threat doesn't sound good. Please let me know if you need my services going forward, of course." Drew leaned forward, more at ease and confident than he came across during his conversation with Lia. "To answer the question: I suppose it depends on how well she knew the law, and how much she wanted to have upon his passing. If she was aware that he was planning to change the will, but wasn't in the mood to fight for her elective share of one-third of his estate, which she would be entitled to as long as they were not separated, then it's possible she could have had motive. Of course I do not represent that family, nor can I answer everything for sure. This is all hypothetical."

"Of course. What about if he suddenly decided to leave a significant share to a new employee in the last year? Would she be able to fight that in court, that perhaps he wasn't of sound mind or unduly influenced somehow? It sounds kind of odd from just from public knowledge of his personality, don't you think?" asked Nicole, wondering about the references to Al Roman that were bandied about in her cafe from the Knitting for Good ladies.

"Again, it's all hypothetical. Have you met his new operations manager, Al Roman?" asked Drew.

"No, not yet anyway."

Drew smiled. He probably figured out what she was planning next. "I don't think I've helped you much, honestly. It's hard to know what Marjorie may have known, though I suppose a woman with that much money probably had someone advising her. And most women in her position would want to inherit the entire estate. Speculation again, of course." Drew smiled again. "Anything else I can help you with?"

Lia had not returned yet, so Nicole wondered if she should bring up her friend's situation. "What's the next course of action for Lia now?"

Drew looked solemn again. "First, she needs to let her mind relax, to see if she has any memories that might be clues. In the meantime I'm also digging through my father's personal effects and hidden files, trying to see if I can find anything." Drew's eyes shifted to the side as he thought. "Let's exchange contact information today, the three of us, so we can keep in touch about this."

"Okay." Nicole accepted Drew's business card, and she reciprocated by handing Drew her own card and Lia's. "Well, I have a feeling I should go rescue Lia from the bathroom. She's probably very upset. I'll escort her out. It might be best."

"Okay, Dr. Capula," said Drew as he stood up.

"Please, you can call me Nicole." She stood up as well. "And thank you for being honest about Lia's parents. I have a feeling she always thought their sudden passing as odd, especially because she was told that her father ran a stop sign. It didn't make sense. You know why?"

"Why?" asked Drew with a puzzled look on his face.

"Because he was the safest driver she's ever known. Good day, Drew."

CHAPTER FOURTEEN

"Why don't we get the cheese plate? Maybe if you nibble on something with the wine, you'll feel a little better," suggested Nicole. She eyed her dear friend, who looked absolutely distraught. Lia mustered a nod. Their meeting with Drew Blackburn had been so shocking, or at least the nature of what he told them was. Lia's parents, murdered? What kind of secret did her father know? And how much did the CIA investigate?

Lia couldn't handle meeting her clients after what she learned that afternoon, so she rescheduled her meetings. It was for the best. Besides, Nicole realized that Lia wasn't really up to driving anywhere, so they left Lia's car at the lawyer's office. Meanwhile, Nicole drove to the Rosewood Hotel.

Nicole was about to take Lia all the way back to her house, but Lia objected as they passed the hotel, not wanting to interfere with Nicole's original intent for the trip out. Instead, Nicole got the brainstorm to splurge for a room, figuring it gave them more reason to hang around the hotel anyway and ask questions. She wanted to meet both Winston James and Al Roman if possible.

Nicole hoped that resting in a luxury bathrobe, while having room service for a change, might help Lia feel better, or at least give her some time to compose herself. The room service delivery had arrived quite quickly fortunately, but Lia barely nibbled on the cheese and crackers. She kept staring off into space. Nicole turned the television on for her friend, knowing Lia often coped with her stress by watching shows.

"Why don't you rest here for a while. Eat some of the cheese and crackers and zone out a bit. I want to take a look at the ballroom and lounge area downstairs and see if I can find our Winston James. I'm starting to think we're missing something on that one." Nicole looked at her friend sympathetically. She really didn't know what to do or how to support her.

"You know what's weird?" asked Lia.

"What's that?"

"I actually feel better in a way. At least it makes more sense. You know I like things to make sense. Math makes sense to me. Accounting makes sense to me. My father running a stop sign never made sense to me." Lia shook her head and grimaced.

"That crossed my mind, too."

"Okay, go ahead. I'll be okay. This was a good idea, actually. I need a change of environment and at least we're not far from home. Go see what you can find out." Nicole hugged her friend and went into the hallway. She thought about the news with Lia and wanted to tell Dean about it, but realized she couldn't. This time it was different. This was personal to Lia. Maybe at some point she would get permission to tell him from Drew Blackburn and Lia, but not yet. Perhaps Dean would have some insight from his FBI days. On a slightly different note, however—since Dean and Nicole were in a relationship now—she felt the obligation to be honest about her whereabouts, especially since she was going to visit the murder scene. She decided to send Dean a text: *Meeting with lawyer went well. Lia wasn't feeling well after, so she is resting in a room at the Rosewood Hotel. I'm going to take a look at ballroom downstairs.*

She knew he wouldn't like it, but looking, perhaps even admiring, the ballroom in the functioning hotel wasn't necessarily such a strange thing. Except that a murder occurred there.

Nicole approached the elevator down the hall. She was on the sixth floor and needed to get to the first. She definitely didn't want to go up and down the stairs in heels. Besides, she was taking in the whole experience. She pressed the button for floor one and felt a soft pull at her stomach as she descended. When she exited the elevator, she spotted the lobby. The hotel employees looked pretty busy since check-in had just started in the last hour. She wasn't sure which one Winston James was (the man who checked them in had *Paul* on his nametag), or if he was even on duty, but decided she was best off to explore the ballroom first while no one could bother her. She was concerned the ballroom might be locked, but she was surprised to find one of the doors slightly ajar. She entered and closed the door, hoping she wouldn't be interrupted.

Inside the magnificent ballroom by herself, she realized how one could be easily swallowed up in it. She again felt the magic of being in that room— seeing New York City in the distance, especially as night approached—but then she remembered someone was killed there.

She walked inside and stood in the center of the room, hoping to recreate New Year's Eve in her mind. She recalled pointing out Phil Martini to Lia the other night, and tried to conjure the memory in full detail. She walked over to the spot where Phil Martini sat. She was lucky that the tables were still in the same arrangement as the other evening. It didn't look like anything had been moved, even though the police had completed what they needed to do at the scene of the crime. As she sat there, and considered she was exactly where the scene of the crime was, she shuddered.

She stood up and walked near the spot where Phil Martini's body had been sprawled out. Nicole thought about the direction his body had been facing, where his head was. Would that mean anything? The odd part was, he was heading in the direction of the wall, not the entrance to the ball-room. Did he not see his killer and he was simply getting up? Otherwise, he should have been heading to the dance floor or even better, the lobby, for safety. Though the door to the lobby was a number of tables away, heading in its direction still would have been safer than getting cornered near a wall.

She kept thinking about what Lia said upstairs in the room, about making sense. She decided to take a closer look at the wall, to see if she was missing something. There were several large mirrors, nearly floor-to-ceiling, with gorgeous sconces between them. Nothing out of the ordinary. *Maybe he just had bad luck*, she thought.

But she wanted it to make sense.

She took a deep breath and decided to stand where Phil's head had rested, recreating the exact spot where he took his last breaths. At that moment she realized what was unique about that point. For one thing, he would have been able to see the killer behind him with the gun because of the mirror. But there was something else. There was just the slightest shimmer in one of the mirrors, in the shape of a very faint, small circle. She inched forward and then couldn't see it. Then she backed up, and could see it. Odd. She made a mental note of where the circle was by moving forward in a straight line herself, careful to keep the line in her mind. When she arrived at the mirror, seeing her own eyes right in front of her, she decided to touch the exact spot she held in her mind's eye. She felt silly doing so, but she couldn't figure out what kind of circle it was or what would have caused it. Perhaps it was just a defect in the mirror, but at the same time, it was quite coincidental that Phil's body was located exactly where he would have been able to see it, just like Nicole.

She removed her finger from the spot after pressing on it. Suddenly, the mirror shifted, and the entire section of wall moved, producing a small sliver. Nicole was dumbfounded. Could it be a secret room? Now Phil's location on New Year's Eve made sense! Of course, he would have special access to a location if needed. The only problem was, he didn't get there in time. And that must have been because he didn't expect the murderer to kill him. It must have been a surprise attack—someone he never anticipated—and the second he realized it, he was too late.

"I see you found the secret room!" Nicole's heart started to race. Someone found her, and it was before she could get inside. She wasn't sure what she was dealing with, nor did she know what was inside the room or if it was even a safe place to be, so she turned around to see who it was. "I'm Winston James, the concierge. I understand you and

Lia Gibbiano are staying with us. Can I help you with anything?"

Nicole didn't want to seem suspicious, not knowing anything about Winston, so she said, "Lia isn't feeling well. I came downstairs to see if there's a gift shop where I could buy aspirin for her, but then I remembered the horrific evening we had the other night and just wanted to take a moment of silence here. Then I thought my eyes were playing tricks on me and I pressed the mirror and this happened! What is this place?" said Nicole. She hoped she was doing a good job of outwitting Winston James by seeming naive, but she wasn't so sure.

"It's off-limits," he said in a loud voice. "You're Don's friend, aren't you?" asked Winston.

"I'm Nicole, the owner of the Cannoli Cafe in town. Don plays chess there every week, that's all."

"Well, the guy is a murderer. I would hope you're not friends with someone like that," said Winston with an air of disgust. "And to think my mother had dated him at one point. Disgusting."

Nicole eyed the blond twenty-five year old man in front of her. Somehow she expected someone older for his title, though she had experienced the same prejudice when she was a high-level manager in her 20s years ago. "My boyfriend is a private investigator who works with the police department. Trust me, I want justice and if Don is proven to be the murderer, I would find that very upsetting indeed." She felt awkward using the word *boyfriend* but hoped she was convincing.

"Would you now?" Winston approached Nicole. The way he walked towards her gave her the impression he was trying to intimidate her. He stared directly into her eyes with a clenched jaw and then paused.

"Oh, of course! I understand you heard Don talking on the phone with Max and that he asked him to bring a gun. I find that so upsetting. I just didn't want to believe it." Coincidentally, Nicole felt her own phone vibrating in her bag accompanied by the sound of a beep just then. "Excuse me, I just want to make sure this isn't Lia." She reached for her phone, which didn't seem to phase Winston, and realized Dean sent a text message saying: *I'm on my way with Det. Spencer. Winston James lied about the call. Phone company has no record of Don calling Max or vice-versa. Don't go near him. Stay in room with Lia.* Nicole felt all the blood drain her face just then.

"Everything okay?"

Nicole decided her best bet was not to look

alarmed, but instead ask for Al Roman. Besides, maybe Winston wasn't the murderer. And she didn't get to see what was inside that room yet. "Oh, yeah, it was just my boyfriend. He's expecting to hear from me soon. Actually, I wanted to say hello to Al Roman. I know my cousin knew Phil well and I just wanted to get acquainted with his new operations manager. Can you take me to him?"

Winston raised his eyebrows the slightest bit.

"About catering opportunities. I do provide baked goods to parties."

Winston grunted. "Okay. Right this way." He led her out of the ballroom, into the kitchen area, and then through a hallway that led to a set of offices. "Al, someone wants to see you. Good day, ma'am." And with that he gave the slightest smirk.

"Hello, can I help you?" asked a tall, broad-shouldered man, perhaps about fifty years old.

"Yes, I'm Tony Capula's cousin, Nicole! I just wanted to introduce myself. I'm the owner of the Cannoli Cafe in town," she said, hoping she could pull off the conversation after leaving the strange encounter with Winston.

"Oh, yes! I've heard a lot about you. Tony's a great guy," he said with a warm smile.

"Yes, and I'm sorry about the death of your

owner, Phil Martini. It's very upsetting. I was actually in the ballroom when it happened." Nicole was curious to see his reaction.

Al hung his head. "Phil was a great boss. Taught me everything I know. I mean, I ran businesses before. But he took it to the next level, you know?" His eyes moistened.

Nicole's heart went out to him. This did not seem like someone who manipulated an old man into willing him a business, that was for sure. Besides, Phil was still fairly astute. It was tough to imagine him being swindled.

She decided to take a chance. "Al, I'm sorry for being so forward but I just had a strange encounter with one of your employees. I was just in the ballroom earlier when Winston came in. Did you know there is a secret room there, accessible from one of the mirrors? I didn't see the inside, but I realized that Phil Martini was just a few feet away from saving himself possibly, if only he had made it to that room." Nicole's voice sounded pained, realizing how Phil could have narrowly escaped death, but didn't. "Was it a panic room?"

Al's warm disposition shifted to one of alarm. His eyes grew wide. "No one is supposed to know about that room, especially not the employees." He shook his head and came around from the desk. "That was to protect Phil if needed. A place for him to escape to if someone went postal around here, or if someone was after him. Was Winston surprised?"

"I'm sorry, he came up from behind and startled me. He didn't seem surprised in the least and instead told me it's off limits. I got the impression he already knew about it." Nicole cocked her head, waiting to see Al's reaction.

"Don't go anywhere, I'll be right back." Al raced out of his office, shutting the door loudly on his way out. Nicole was stunned. What was she really dealing with here? Was Winston the murderer after all?

She kept thinking about the secret room and the placement of Phil's body, and the fact that he was too late. *The murderer must have been a party guest if he didn't suspect anything earlier*, she thought. But how did no one have a gun on them in the ballroom when Phil's body was found? Did they really escape or did they just blend in with the guests?

Nicole took her phone out and called the cafe. "Susie, is Celeste still there? I need to speak with her. It's important." Susie asked her to hold while she got Celeste.

"Hello, Nicole? This is Celeste."

"Celeste, you mentioned your table was toward the back the other night at the party. Can you tell me who screamed and where that person was standing when Phil's body was discovered?" asked Nicole.

"Oh, it was Don Martini's date, Clarisa. I remember seeing her face clearly because her back was to the wall." Nicole gasped. She knew right then that Clarisa was the murderer.

Suddenly, she heard the doorknob slowly turn to Al's office. *No one turns a doorknob slowly if it's their own office*, she thought. She kept the phone on but put it in her bag, leaving the bag half-open as the door opened all the way.

In walked Clarisa with a gun in her hand, aimed directly at Nicole.

CHAPTER FIFTEEN

"Don't shoot!" yelled Nicole, hoping someone on the other line heard her. "Al is coming right back, Clarisa."

"Oh no, he isn't. He's busy with Winston in that secret room right now. Al won't be here for a while, I'm sure. I'll guess they'll find your dead body eventually."

And then it hit Nicole. Why Clarisa was doing this.

"But I don't understand why you're pointing the gun at me, Clarisa. What did I do to you?" She fibbed.

Clarisa laughed. "Give me a break. Why don't *you* tell me why I have to kill you!"

Nicole held her head steady. "Because I figured out how you killed Phil Martini the other night."

"Ahh. Let me hear it," she said with a sadistic smile.

"Winston James, the concierge of this hotel, was a bellhop two years ago. The same bellhop that helped Phil Martini during the minor earthquake. And he became the only employee to ever see the safe room, except for the new operations manager Al Roman."

"Go on." Clarisa kept smiling.

"Though he was saved during the earthquake, Phil didn't like that Winston knew about the safe room, so he blackmailed him. He made him concierge and paid him well in exchange for his silence. Keeping him at the hotel was also a way he could watch him closely."

"I'm still waiting to hear the part about me, dearie," said Clarisa.

"I'm getting to it. I'm sure Phil thought Winston had left the hotel New Year's Eve when his shift completed at midnight. What he didn't expect, however, was that Winston would tell his mother, *you*, about the room, so that you could stash the gun there after firing it." Nicole saw Clarisa's eyebrows raise the slightest bit. "I thought it was interesting when Winston mentioned his mother having dated Don."

"What else did you figure out?" asked Clarisa.

"That you killed Phil while his will still named Don as one of his beneficiaries, in addition to his wife, Marjorie. You figured Don would be marrying you soon, and that you'd inherit everything he owns as his wife," said Nicole.

Clarisa's jaw clenched. "And how did you figure that part out, exactly?"

"Let's just say I got a tip that he was about to change his will. And everyone assumed that meant cutting Marjorie's share down and dealing Al in. But actually, Phil and Don were fighting because Phil knew he had to change the will if Don married you. Because Phil didn't want Winston's mother to inherit anything of his." Nicole took a breath. "Unfortunately, he underestimated you and never expected you to kill him, especially practically in front of everyone at New Year's Eve. And he never thought Winston would sell him out since he was compensating him so well."

"I must admit, you are pretty smart." Clarisa raised her eyebrows. "So, where is Oliver Pierson in all this?"

"Ah, well part of what you and Max told me

was true, though I'm sure it all came from you.
Jeannette did take the private loan record from
Phil's office during the supposed break-in, but not
with any intention to kill. She and Oliver wanted to
blackmail Phil about the other names on it. So if it
was in their possession they could get out of paying
the rest of the loan back." Nicole bit her lip. "And I
bet Winston had a fairly sizable loan that didn't
need to be repaid as long as he kept his mouth shut
about the room, right?"

Clarisa's eyes widened as Nicole continued.
"So, you had to execute a double-murder. You had
to kill Phil to get what you wanted from his will.
And even if Don didn't marry you, though he
probably would have, you protected your son from
what Oliver might have done in light of his knowledge and possession of the loan record. So you tore
off the part of the record that had Winston's name
on it and left the part with Oliver's name with his
dead body." Nicole continued. "The beauty of your
plan was, it wouldn't make sense on the outside.
Why expose the loans if you hoped to inherit the
estate in some part, since it could have opened up a
can of worms with the government. Perhaps a
minor inconvenience since you'd be inheriting such
a large pie anyhow. But on the other hand, if you

killed the person who had the loan document in their possession and got control over it, your son would be protected and the police would suspect others with loans might have killed Phil." Nicole paused.

"And the part with Winston accusing Don of killing his brother?" asked Clarisa.

"That was just a red herring to get the police to spend their energy looking in the wrong places." Nicole shook her head.

"Music to my ears. Such a great plan, right? It was like chess. All the pieces got in the right position for me to capture the king." Clarisa seemed absolutely pleased with herself. "But no one else knows this or has figured it out. Only you have, Nicole. And if something happens to you, no one would understand why or how. There are no cameras in this building. It will simply be a mystery. Any last words?" Nicole panicked. She realized no one was coming after all. Maybe Susie or Celeste hung the phone up or couldn't hear the conversation.

Suddenly, Nicole heard a voice through the crack of the door. "You are surrounded, Clarisa. Put your weapon down, hands up. We have your son here." Clarisa grimaced and put her gun down. Detective Spencer from the police force rushed in.

They opened the door all the way, and Nicole rushed out when she saw Dean in the hallway.

He grabbed her and gave her a hug. "Thank goodness you called the cafe. Susie and Celeste heard everything!" Dean pulled back to look at Nicole and then gave her a soft kiss on the lips. "Are you okay?"

Nicole smiled. "I am now."

EPILOGUE

"HEY, PROFESSOR! WHERE'S MY SPAGHETTI?" yelled Don Martini, followed by a hearty laugh.

"Oh no, Mr. Martini! Don't tell me your old grumpy self is back! I was starting to like the new *Don*!" Everyone laughed. Susie was throwing a little "coffee and cannolis" reception for Nicole at the cafe, to help celebrate her safe return.

Don shook his head. "I'm sorry, everyone. I feel like such a dumb old fool. I guess it was too good to be true that an attractive, younger woman would be so interested in me!"

"That's okay, Don. But you do have a lot of true friends here in Rosewood. Don't forget that!" Nicole winked at Max. He smiled back.

"Now, do you guys think you can keep my daughter away from trouble while we're in Texas? We're leaving this weekend!" said John Capula. "Dean, in case you missed the memo, I'm talking to you!" Anna looked stunned as her husband addressed Dean.

Dean flushed bright red. "I will try, sir, but you know she has a mind of her own. I can't control her and I wouldn't dare try!"

Lia piped up. "Nicole certainly has a knack for figuring this stuff out. She's getting better and better at it!" Lia looked over and Nicole felt a small chill. She knew what Lia was getting at, that perhaps she could help solve the mystery of her parents' death.

"There's one piece I don't understand, Nicole. How did Clarisa manage to kill Oliver Pierson at the gallery?" asked Don.

"Yes, I was wondering about that part too, actually," added Susie.

Dean shifted in his chair. "I can explain that one. Clarisa dressed up in a wig and server uniform, compliments of her son stealing a black waitstaff uniform from the hotel, to help blend in at the party. Then she told Oliver there was something he needed to see upstairs, that it would concern him as the gallery owner."

"But how did she get the loan document from him?" asked Don.

"You know, she took a gamble—she figured something as important as that paper would stay on Oliver's person, and she was right." Dean took a breath. "Too bad Jeannette had coincidentally taken me aside right before that to talk about my art instructor's piece while Marjorie cornered Nicole in the ladies' room. It was perfect timing for Clarisa to strike."

"She was clever, I'll give her that," said Nicole. "And it wasn't even Don's gun, right? She had gotten her own gun and silencer out-of-state?"

"That's right. She stole Don's gun and hid it in the safe room, just to throw the investigation off at first. She figured she would let it resurface at some point so that the case would get thrown out and then she'd marry Don and inherit the estate through marriage." He looked over at Nicole. "Clarisa mentioned she knew how smart Nicole was, but Clarisa still underestimated her. If it weren't for Nicole finding that room and the confrontation in Al's office, she might have gotten away with all of it!"

"Unbelievable!" said Don. "Just, unbelievable. Not to mention that it was a tag-team effort. Mother and son. She couldn't have pulled it off without Winston's help."

"I know. That was a bit of a twist, too. Well, we'll have to put it behind us now, Don. It's a shame, but it *is* a new year. Time to start looking forward!" said Nicole.

Suddenly, Celeste appeared from the kitchen. "Would anyone like cookies? Fresh out of the oven!"

"Everyone, I'd like you to meet Celeste. She is our newest employee." Nicole smiled broadly. "And I'm also officially hiring Lia on a part-time basis to handle the books."

"Welcome, Celeste and Lia! Wow, Nicole, you're really doing well with this cafe!" remarked her father, John.

"Well, I have big plans this year and need the help." Dean's eyes widened as Nicole looked over at him and took his hand. "My new year's resolution is to make more time for my relationships and friendships. The past year was definitely a tough transition out of industry, but I'm ready to start focusing more on my personal life." Dean's face lit up.

Nicole's mother, Anna, chimed in. "I think

that's a wise decision, sweetheart. We all love you and want the best for you. Happy New Year, honey!"

Everyone raised their Cannoli Cafe mugs and in unison shouted, "Happy New Year!"

RECIPES

These recipes are included for fun. Feel free to experiment with them. As always, please use caution and be mindful of kitchen/culinary safety practices!

Roasted Asparagus Wrapped with Prosciutto

This is a nice, easy recipe to use as a starter or side dish!

Ingredients:

    1 lb. asparagus

    1 tablespoon olive oil

    ½ lb. prosciutto, thinly sliced

    Salt and pepper

1. Preheat the oven to 400 deg F.

2. Remove the dry stems off of each stalk
    of asparagus (cut or snap). Place each
    stem on a greased baking sheet (olive oil
    spray is fine). Drizzle the asparagus with
    olive oil, sprinkle salt and pepper on top,
    and then toss. Place the baking sheet in
    the oven for fifteen minutes. Then
    remove the sheet and allow the
    asparagus to cool completely.

3. Wrap each asparagus with 1 piece of
    prosciutto (or half a slice) of prosciutto,
    leaving the tips exposed. Arrange and
    serve at room temperature.

Italian Pot Roast with Porcini Mushrooms

*This is a nice dish to serve for special occasions that is
not too difficult to make. Serves 6-8.*

Ingredients:

1 (5 lb.) boneless beef chuck roast

2 onions (chopped)

6 cloves of garlic (crushed)

1 cup red wine

¼ cup olive oil total

1 (15 oz.) can beef broth (can be low-sodium)

$\frac{1}{2}$ oz. dried porcini mushrooms

1 sprigs' fresh rosemary leaves, chopped

6 sprigs' worth of fresh thyme leaves, chopped

Salt and pepper

1. Preheat the oven to 350 deg F.
2. Season the beef with salt and pepper. In a 6-quart dutch oven, heat 2 tablespoons of olive oil over medium-high heat. Add the beef and brown on all sides. Remove the beef and set aside.
3. Reduce the heat to medium. Add the remaining oil and onions. Cook until tender. Add the garlic for one minute. Then add the wine. If possible, use a wooden spoon to scrape the bottom of the dutch oven. Stir in the broth and mushrooms. Cover the pot and transfer to the oven. Cook until fork-tender, about 3 hours. Turn the beef over halfway through and add more broth if needed.
4. Remove the dutch oven carefully from the oven. Transfer the beef to a 9x13 dish and tent with foil.
5. Use an immersion blender to blend the

pan juices and vegetables in the dutch oven. Then add rosemary and thyme. Heat the sauce until it's simmering (for 5 minutes). Add salt and pepper if needed. Alternatively, you can transfer the contents into a blender and use that instead before heating the sauce.

6. Add the sauce to the beef and serve!

Note that you can cut the beef into pieces if you'd like, however I find that it's so tender you don't really need a knife. I leave it after I put the pan sauce on the beef and simply serve from the 9x13 dish.

AUTHOR'S NOTE

The Cannoli Cafe Mystery Series is inspired by my Italian-American upbringing in New Jersey (my mother's family is Italian and I grew up very close to them; I spent a lot of time at my grandparents' house growing up, enjoying traditional Italian cooking). This particular book is reminiscent of the many Italian New Year's Eve parties I attended in the past, where the whole ballroom is full of joy with many "whole-room" dances such as the Tarantella!

While the aforementioned elements are true of my own life, the entire story and all the characters are fictional, and any coincidences to any particular events or anything else are just that—coincidental and fictional.

I sincerely hope you enjoyed my fourth work of fiction, and if you'd like to be notified when my next book comes out, please visit:

http://lizziebenton.com.

Also, you are welcome to follow my Goodreads Author Page .

Thank you again for reading!

amazon.com/author/lizziebenton

goodreads.com/lizziebenton

ALSO BY LIZZIE BENTON

Cannoli Cafe Mystery Series

Murder and Macaroons

Murder and Macaroni

Iced Cookie Murder